We passed under a drooping willow tree near the bridge.

"Stop." I cried furiously. "This is as far as I'm going!"

"Yes, my dear!" Once again he uttered his strange, malevolent laugh. "This *is* as far as you are going!"

"Let go of me!" I cried, and tried to wrench my arm away, but still he held me tight. As I gaped at the man who was holding me, a scream rose to my throat, to be clamped back as he rammed a rolled-up handkerchief into my mouth with his free hand, and I found myself staring, petrified. . . .

Now, too late, the memory of Ivy's description of her assailant came back to me. . . .

IN LOVE, IN VIENNA

Daisy Thomson

A JOVE/HBJ BOOK

First Jove/HBJ edition published October 1977

Library of Congress Catalog Card Number: 77-80695

Printed in the United States of America

Jove/HBJ books are published by Jove Publications, Inc.
(Harcourt Brace Jovanovich) 757 Third Avenue, New York,
N.Y. 10017

Chapter One

I was about to get into bed when the telephone buzzed discreetly. I gaped at the instrument in surprise, wondering who on earth would be calling me at one o'clock in the morning. In fact, apart from my parents, who knew to locate me at the Mahler Hotel in Vienna?

At the thought of my parents my heart missed a beat. A telephone call at this time of night could mean only one thing. Either my mother or my father had taken ill! Perhaps there had been an accident!

Shakily I grabbed at the receiver. "Yes?" I tried to be calm. "Miranda Ogilvie speaking. Who is it?"

"Miss Ogilvie! Thank goodness you are still awake!" an almost hysterical voice gabbled at me. "I do so need someone to talk to! Someone to turn to for advice! You have no idea of the shock I have just had!"

I gritted my teeth, convinced now that a fellow delegate at the International Novelists Conference I was attending was playing a joke on me, trying to introduce a note of melodrama into the conventional atmosphere of the congress.

"Who is speaking, please?" I demanded crossly.

"It's Ivy! Ivy Sikorska!" the brittle, excited voice announced. "The most peculiar thing happened to me less than ten minutes ago! At first I could not believe it, and I simply have to talk it over with someone, and you struck me as being such a sympathetic and sensible young woman, I was sure you wouldn't mind if I appealed to you."

I took a deep breath to control my annoyance. This silly, middle-aged, head-in-the-clouds colleague of mine had no right to telephone me at this ungodly hour, to pour out her woes and imaginative upsets.

I should have taken Senga Watson's advice and steered clear of Ivy, but she had looked so helpless and dithery and alone at the official reception in the evening that I had felt sorry for her, and spent quite some time with her—and this was my reward!

I sighed at my foolishness as I remembered what Senga had said to me on the flight from London as we sat chatting together.

"That's Ivy Sikorska sitting down the aisle from us," she nodded her head to indicate the woman she was talking about. "Whatever you do, Miranda, steer clear of her! I know that this is your first conference with the Association, and I don't want it to be spoilt for you. The rest of us have had to suffer Ivy in the past, and believe me, she is an impossible woman!

"Ivy is a clinger, like her name." She went on to describe the very successful romantic novelist, about whom I already knew some biographical details from the back covers of her books. "She will tag on to you, Miranda, because you are new, and everyone else will be doing their best to avoid her!"

"She is not only a clinger," interrupted Mabel

Angus, who was seated at my other side. "She makes use of people, and she has absolutely no scruples about anything. Be warned! Don't discuss your future plots with her, she will use them all herself, without a qualm! I vow that she has risen to her present success by picking other people's brains!"

"And don't ever invite her to join you for a coffee, or to sit at your dinner table," put in Senga again. "You will find you will be left to foot the bill, because Ivy hadn't had time to cash her traveler's checks!"

While my two new friends had been speaking, I had been glancing down the aisle of the plane to have a look at the woman they were discussing, who was talking nineteen to the dozen with her neighbor.

Ivy Sikorska was an eye-catching figure, with her black cossack hat, her long black coat trimmed with black fur at neck and hemline, and black leather boots. Long, pendant jet earrings drooped from the white lobes of her fleshy ears, and the wiry tendrils of hair that escaped from under her hat were as black as the swinging jet baubles. The high collar of the coat emphasized the powdered whiteness of her cheeks, and her lips were two bold lines of vivid scarlet under her long, aristocratic nose.

"I was wondering who she was when I saw her in the departure lounge," I remarked to Senga. "She looked as if she had stepped straight from the pages of _Dr. Zhivago!_"

"Her latest novel is based on the Nicholas and Alexandra theme," Mabel remarked. "I wonder

7

what she would dress like if she used a South Seas background," she added waspishly.

I didn't know Mabel or Senga very well, and I thought they were merely being rather bitchy about an older woman who had achieved more success than they had in the writing world.

A few hours later, having spent a wearisome evening, or more accurately part of an evening, being polite to her at the reception given to our delegation by the Ministry of Education in the Palais Palffy, I appreciated why they felt about her as they did, and also why even some of the delegates from other countries wryly referred to her as "Poison Ivy"!

What I now regretted most of all was giving my room number to her, in response to her anxious plea.

"My dear Miss Ogilvie! I get so nervous in strange hotels, especially in a country where I don't speak the language. It would be such a comfort to me if I knew what room you were in. If I felt ill, or some other emergency arose, I could contact you."

She certainly had not wasted any time in thinking up an emergency, I thought with annoyance as her voice gabbled on and on over the wires.

"I tell you, Miss Ogilvie," she was saying. "It was him! I just couldn't be mistaken. When you have lived with a man for five years you can't mistake him! It was Jan all right, and I am quite sure he recognized me too!"

"Mrs. Sikorska," I interrupted her. "I'm sorry. I have had a long day, and I'm tired out. I was just getting into bed when you telephoned. Couldn't whatever you want to talk to me about wait until morning?"

"No, Miss Ogilvie, no!" she wailed. "Please, please listen to me now! What happened is so incredible I simply have to talk to someone about it!"

"You were saying something about your husband," I said wearily.

"Yes! I was trying to tell you, but you kept interrupting me!" her voice rose hysterically. "I saw Jan less than ten minutes ago, in the hotel elevator!"

So what? I stifled a yawn. Why was Ivy so excited about seeing her husband? Hadn't she known he was coming to Vienna? And why make a song and dance about his appearance to me, at this time of night?

"So you saw your husband," I tried to sound interested. "Didn't you expect him to be here?"

She choked over her next words, indignation at my lack of knowledge of her much publicized background struggling with excitement over what had happened.

"Miss Ogilvie!" she squawked. "My husband was reported missing, believed killed, in a raid over Berlin more than thirty years ago! I have believed him to be dead all that time, and now, this very night, I have seen him again!"

"Oh!" I was dumbfounded. "Oh!" I repeated. "Mrs. Sikorska, you couldn't have! You imagined a likeness! This has been an exciting day . . ." I hurried on, tactfully making no mention of the fact that she had also imbibed rather a lot of the potent Austrian wine that had been served freely at the Palais reception, and in the state she had been in when I had left her there, she could have imagined anything!

"I tell you, it was my husband I saw! I followed this man into the elevator, and as he turned to press the button to take him up to his floor, we looked directly into each other's eyes, and it was Jan! I called him by name, and he looked taken aback!"

I tried not to giggle. Tonight Ivy had worn a black lace evening dress, with a hobble skirt, which reflected the style of the Edwardian era. Ropes of black beads formed a choker at her neck and spilled down over her ample bosom. Her wiry, unnaturally black hair was piled on top of her head and skewered precariously into position with an ornamental comb, and her beady, birdlike brown eyes had been boldly outlined with dark pencil. It was small wonder that the unfortunate stranger she had hailed as her husband had been taken aback!

"Yes, he was very taken aback, and very worried." Ivy uttered a peculiar laugh. "So worried that it started off his nervous tic!"

"His nervous tic?" I echoed.

"Yes. When Jan was upset about something, he seemed to lose the power of controlling the muscles of his left eyelid, so that it would twitch and droop over his eye, almost closing it—and that is exactly what happened tonight! That's how I was sure it was Jan!"

"You mean, he recognized you too?" I sighed, thinking what hard luck it was for the man, if he was Jan Sikorski, to fall into Ivy's clutches again, after thirty-odd years of freedom from her demanding ways!

"He recognized me all right," exclaimed Ivy indignantly, "but he pretended not to! When the elevator stopped at the next floor, to let more people in, he waited until the doors were about to close again, before pushing his way out after the other man who had entered the elevator with us, and almost knocking him over in his hurry, much to the other fellow's indignation! Then, before I could follow, the doors closed and I was whisked up to the next floor, and lost sight of him!"

Ivy's story was becoming too far-fetched to be believable.

"Listen, Mrs. Sikorska," I said briskly. "Apparently you have seen someone you think resembles your late husband. It gave you a shock, and you then let your rather vivid imagination run away with you."

"You don't believe me, do you, Miss Ogilvie?" she interrupted me with bitterness in her voice. "I don't suppose anyone else will either, unless I can track him down and confront him, and that is precisely what I am going to do! He is bound to be staying in this hotel, and I shall telephone the receptionist right away and ask her for his room number!"

"You do that, Mrs. Sikorska," I yawned. "It will set your mind at rest when you find out that there is not a Mr. Sikorski staying here. Also," I tried to sound more sympathetic, "you sound so strung up that I think you should take

11

a sleeping pill or something to calm your nerves, or you will not be able to rest tonight."

"A sleeping pill!" she repeated, scandalized. "I have never taken a sleeping pill or a tranquilizer in my life. Even when I heard the news of poor Jan's death, I refused the doctor's offer of one, and I am certainly not going to take one when I have found out that he is still alive!"

"Goodnight, Mrs. Sikorska," I sighed, "I—"

Before I could finish my sentence, she slammed down her receiver with an indignant bang which set my ears ringing.

I replaced my own receiver and crept into bed, thinking as I did so that poor Ivy had been writing so many fictitious adventures that she no longer seemed to know where reality stopped and fantasy started!

I stretched out my arm and switched off the bedlight, before snuggling cosily under the covers. I wanted to weave my own dreams tonight. I was young, I was fancy-free, I was in Vienna, city of dreams and romance, and there was that very attractive and amusing young man I had met at the Palais Palffy, after I had sneaked away from Ivy, to think about, to say nothing of the elderly, hand-kissing baron who had flirted outrageously with me while his wife looked benignly on, amused rather than upset by his capers.

I was smiling as I drifted off to sleep, wondering if Phil Hunter would get in touch with me in the morning, as he had promised, or if he had met another young woman to flirt with after I had left the reception. Ivy and her problems were far from my mind as I closed my eyes, and they were still far from it when I woke shortly after eight o'clock the following morning and slipped out of bed, to cross over the carpeted floor and pull back the heavily lined curtains which covered the floor-to-ceiling picture windows.

I stretched myself as I stood, looking out from my eleventh-storey window over the rooftops of Vienna. A pale golden sun was struggling to dispel the November mists, which lingered in the valleys of the streets and along the railway line which snaked far below me. Church spires pointed up towards the clearing sky, and over the house tops, like sinister, lost spirits, great black crows cawed dismally, and wheeled around and around each other, and around the chimney tops, and in and out of the leafless trees which lined the avenues.

The crows gave me a curious feeling of uneasiness. There was something ominous, something threatening about the way they swooped and darted; something weird and other-worldly about their raucous cries.

With a shudder of distaste I stepped back from the window and turned my back on them, but their cries still echoed in my ears, recalling to my mind Ivy's sharp, hysterical voice on the phone in the middle of the night, when she had poured into my ears her improbable story of a husband who had come back from the dead!

Chapter Two

I peeled off the deep hyacinth-blue nylon night-gown I was wearing, flung it negligently on the bed, and walked the length of the enormous bedroom to the bathroom which was to the left of the corridor which led to the bedroom door.

The Mahler management had thoughtfully provided packets of bath foam essence, which I emptied into the steaming water, and soon a pleasant aroma of pine filled the little room. I stepped into the bath and luxuriated in the soft, sweet-smelling water. This was the life, I sighed blissfully. This was much, much better than taking a hasty shower before hurriedly dressing and darting out into the raw, cold morning air of Edinburgh, to catch the bus which would take me to the library where I worked, as I had been doing at this time only three days ago, and would be doing again, for weeks on end, when the Vienna Conference was over.

I was zipping up the back of the honey-gold angora wool dress I had eventually decided to wear that day, when there was a knock at the door, and a waiter came in carrying the breakfast tray.

"*Guten Morgen*, Fräulein!" he greeted me with a smile and a polite bow as he set it down on the large round table beside the window, where he stood waiting for me to sign a chit for it, before with another bow and an admiring smile, he turned and left the room.

I sat eating my breakfast in solitary splendor, while the worldly-wise eyes of a Gustav Klimt courtesan stared unblinkingly down at me from the print which hung above the huge bed on which I had slept so comfortably last night—a bed which could have accommodated at least four people in comfort, and in which I had been able to toss and turn freely. At home, my freedom of movement is restricted by the fact that the two family cats insist on sleeping at the foot of my bed, and are inclined to pounce painfully on my toes if I make too many disturbing movements!

I was pouring out my second cup of coffee when the telephone buzzed, reminding me instantly of the odd conversation I had had with Ivy Sikorska in the early hours of the morning.

I stiffened, and some of the euphoria I had been feeling dissipated.

Damn! I muttered to myself. I must not let Ivy assume that I was at her beck and call all the time. I would have to tell her so, firmly. I had scrimped and saved to afford to be able to come to this conference, to fulfil a long-cherished desire to return to a city in which I had once stayed for several weeks as a student; a city with which I had fallen in love, and in which I had fallen in love, briefly, lightheartedly, with the son of the household in which I was staying. It would be maddening to have the Sikorska woman hanging around my neck all the time!

I steeled myself to say "No" to her requests, whatever they were, and my voice, as I spoke into the telephone, was cool and unfriendly.

"Yes? Who is speaking, please?"

15

"My, my!" an amused male voice said. "You sound as if you had got out of bed on the wrong side this morning, Miranda! Didn't you sleep well last night?"

"Phil!" I exclaimed, and there was delight, not harshness in my tone. "Thank goodness! At first I thought you might be 'Poison Ivy', and I very nearly didn't answer the phone!"

"Poison Ivy?" he repeated, and I could picture his amused frown as he spoke. "Who on earth is that?"

"She is a fellow British delegate, and a dreadful hanger-on. She was the one you helped me escape from last night!"

"The woman in black, who was holding herself stiff as a ramrod, because she had drunk so much wine?" Phil chuckled.

"That's the one," I agreed, "but I didn't entirely escape from her clutches last night. Do you know, she had the gall to telephone me at one o'clock in the morning, just as I was about to get into bed, to tell me a garbled tale about a long-lost husband, or rather a long-dead husband she had met up with again in the elevator last night!"

I shook my head, remembering the conversation with Ivy, as I added, "But you didn't telephone me to hear about another woman's love life, did you?"

"I telephoned you because I did promise I would get in touch with you again as soon as possible!" he replied.

"Yes, you did!" I smiled joyfully to myself, feeling highly delighted that the man who had interested me so much the previous evening had meant what he said about hoping to meet me again.

"You didn't say if you had made any plans for this morning," went on Phil, "so I was hoping that you would be free to come with me to feed the ducks in the Stadtpark, and let me introduce you to Johann Strauss, before going to Demel's for coffee."

"Phil! That's a program after my own heart! I have never been introduced to Johann Strauss before, and I am looking forward to that pleasure!"

"Good!" Phil Hunter sounded as pleased as I was feeling at my acceptance of his invitation. "I shall meet you at the foot of the flying staircase in the reception hall in ten minutes' time. That should give you time to beautify yourself!"

"I can't decide whether you are flattering me or not with that remark!" I retorted lightly.

"In that case, perhaps I should take a leaf out of your gallant baron's book," he reminded me of the other man who had been dancing attendance on me at the Palais Palffy, "and say that since you are already beautiful, I shall expect you right away?"

"Phil"—I was enjoying our banter—"let's compromise. I shall meet you in the reception hall in five minutes, how about that?"

He agreed, and I hurriedly brushed my gleaming, whiskey-brown hair, renewed my make-up, checked that I had everything I required in my handbag, and put on the sheepskin-lined, tan-colored suede coat which I had extravagantly treated myself to the previous week.

The coat was not only warm, so that it would resist the bitingly cold winds I had been warned swept through Vienna at this time of year, but it was also elegantly fashionable, with its high, red fox fur collar, its nipped-in waist and long flared skirt. It had a luxurious look which gave me the confidence of knowing that I looked well, the kind of confidence all women like to have when they are going to meet a new acquaintance, and especially when they are going for a rendezvous with a handsome and intriguing man!

I pulled a fox fur hat down over my ears, checked in the mirror that I hadn't smudged mascara on my cheek, which I sometimes do when I put on eye make-up in a hurry, and then, satisfied that I looked reasonably attractive, I left the room to take the elevator down to the ground floor.

The admiring look on Phil's face as he came forward to meet me in the reception hall gave me a warm glow of well-being, and for my part I decided that Phil Hunter was even more ruggedly handsome than I had thought him to be the previous evening.

My pulse raced with pleasure as he smiled a greeting and took my room key from me to hand over to the receptionist.

"I hope you saved at least one of your breakfast rolls for the ducks," he remarked as we made our way towards the main exit.

"Oh!" I exclaimed. "I don't have anything for them. I had eaten my breakfast before you telephoned me, and since the rolls were so delicious, especially the salty ones, there wasn't a crumb over!"

"In that case, the poor ducks will have to go hungry this morning!" shrugged Phil. "I'm afraid I ate all mine as well! We shall have to remember not to be so greedy tomorrow morning!"

"Perhaps we shall pass a bakery on the way to the park," I suggested, but Phil shook his head.

"That's the park over there, just across the street. There is one thing," he went on, as he pushed open the door and we went out into the cold, raw November air. "I don't think Johann will expect us to feed him, so we shall pay him our respects now and feed the ducks on our way back to the hotel, with whatever crumbs we leave from our cakes at Demel's!"

Phil tucked his arm in mine as we stood waiting for an opportunity to cross the busy street which lay between us and the Stadtpark. A chill wind blustered against us, and I had to clutch at my hat so that it would not be tugged from my head as we hurried across the road and over the bridge which spans the Vienna River and leads into the gardens.

In spite of the efforts of the sun, wisps of mist still lingered near the river and under the trees. The paths which meandered through the park, revealing at every turn an unexpected statue of a famous Viennese of the past, were damp and often slippery underfoot with the last of the autumn leaves.

Sparrows and blackbirds pecked about the

19

grass and under the low shrubs for food, and the huge crows which I had noticed earlier that day, when I had opened my curtains to let in the morning light, stalked with their ungainly swagger over the lawns, or took off, with noisily swishing wings, to soar back into the air, where they wheeled over our heads calling raucously to one another.

I gave a cry of alarm as one of the crows suddenly swooped down so close to me I could feel the draught of its passing on my cheeks.

"I like birds, Phil," I said with a shiver, "but there is something about those crows which makes me feel ill at ease. They seem like birds of ill omen—and there are so many of them!" I looked around me unhappily. "I remember thinking the same thing on my previous visit to Vienna, when I remarked to a friend that a crow should be incorporated into the city's coat-of-arms!"

"I wonder if there is a connection between the crows and the reason why there are so many Breughels in the Kunsthistorisches Museum?" remarked Phil. "Have you ever noticed that in most of his paintings there are crows or magpies?"

He made a sudden grab at my arm as my heel slipped on a pile of sodden and decaying leaves and I almost fell.

"I think you should keep your eyes on the ground and not on the crows in the sky!" he advised me, smiling. "It would never do if you broke your leg, or your neck, on the first day of your winter holiday in Vienna!"

We walked past the duck pond, and the ducks came waddling hopefully towards us, fluttering their tails and fixing us with their beady eyes, then went quacking away in disgust as we went on our way without giving them a titbit.

"And now, here is the great man himself!" Phil announced as we came up to the Hellmer statue of the King of Waltzes, with his attendant Danube nymphs surrounding him.

"Johann, meet Miranda Ogilvie!" he saluted the statue with a flourish. "Miranda, meet my friend, Johann Strauss; may he inspire you to write as many successful romantic novels as he wrote romantic tunes!"

I laughed. "Heaven forbid! That would be condemning me to a lifetime of hard work! Do you realize that Strauss wrote 496 works of immortal value, as my guidebook puts it, which would mean I would have to write about ten books a year for the next fifty years, if I am spared to live out my allotted span!"

"Then forget what I said," smiled Phil, "and come dance with me instead!"

Ignoring the amused looks of three young children and their mother, he took me in his arms and waltzed me up and down the path in front of the statue, while he blithely hummed the opening bars of the "Blue Danube Waltz."

"Please, Phil!" I said breathlessly, struggling to release myself from his arms. "People will think we are mad, acting like this in broad daylight!"

"No, they won't. Not here in Vienna!" he assured me, but he stopped his capers and let go of me, and walked sedately by my side as we made for the Schubertring and crossed the road to follow an intricate maze of narrow streets and alleyways until we reached the Kohlmarkt, and Demel's world-famous coffee shop.

I was glad to enter the cosy, old-fashioned atmosphere of Demel's. In spite of my warm coat and hat and fur-lined boots, I had been very conscious of the biting wind which swept across the city, and my nose and cheeks ached with the freezing cold.

Phil ordered two cups of Mokka, the strong black Viennese coffee. Since I protested that it was still too early in the day for me to be able to enjoy one of the rich Austrian cakes for which the café is famous, we settled instead for the plainer crescent rolls, rolls which are said to have been first created at the time of Ferdinand I in 1683 by the Viennese bakers who gave the alarm when they heard, near their ovens, the tapping of the Turkish troops who were trying to invade the town through tunnels driven under the ramparts.

I wrapped up half of my roll in a paper serviette, and Phil did the same, in order to have something to give to the ducks on our way back through the park.

We sat for a long time over coffee, for I was in no hurry to go out into the cold again. Moreover, I was curious about Phil Hunter, for although I had told him about myself and my family and my work as a librarian in the university, as well as about my previous visit to Vienna, he had told me very little about himself, except to say that he was in Vienna on business of a private nature.

"Since you are not a delegate at the conference, how did you manage to get into the reception at the Palffy last night?" I asked him.

"I have friends in high places!" he grinned. "The British ambassador was at school with my father!"

"So that's how you managed it!" I nodded. "At first I thought you might be a delegate from the other conference which is being held at the Hilton this week. The one for physicists or scientists or something like that. I saw you talking to one of them in the cocktail bar before my friends and I left for the reception."

"That poor man was glad to talk to someone outside of his learned friends!" Phil smiled. "Unfortunately, he was not allowed to talk to me for long, since he was a Hungarian."

He glanced around the café before he continued.

"These international conferences are not always what they seem on the surface, as I expect you will have found out?"

I shook my head.

"This is my very first such congress, and I can't say I understand what you are driving at."

"You will! Believe me, Miranda, even with your innocuous-seeming bunch of novelists, there is a sort of 'us' and 'them' intrigue going on!

"Those of us from the West are naturally curious to learn what goes on on the other side of the Iron Curtain, and the 'thems' are equally curious about us. In fact, some of them would even like to come and join us permanently," he sipped his coffee thoughtfully. "That is why the East never allows an entire family to come to the West together. Husbands have to leave their wives or children behind. Wives have to leave their children or parents. It is a hostage system, really. What is more, you will find, Miranda, that if you talk to a fellow writer from behind the Curtain for any length of time on your own, someone will come over to check up on what you are discussing, and even suggest to whomever you are speaking, that they are wanted for a word in private!"

I stared at Phil incredulously.

"You are making all this up, aren't you?" I laughed. "I am sure now that you are a fellow writer after all! What's your line? Spy story or pure thriller?" I teased him.

He signaled the waiter without answering my question.

"Come on, Miranda," he stood up. "If you want to have time to feed the ducks before lunch, we had better be on our way. In any case," he added, "I have to be back at the Hilton before mid-day for an appointment."

We walked briskly back along the narrow streets of the old quarter of Vienna, which is contained by the Ringstrassen, and once again crossed the Schubertring and entered the Stadtpark.

We spent a few minutes feeding the ducks and the sparrows and admiring particularly the gorgeous colorings of a stately Mandarin duck, which wanted to follow us back along the path. We shooed him back to the pond and were approaching one of the bridges which crosses the Vienna River when we noticed a crowd of people had gathered there, with several policemen shouting at the crowd to stand back.

Now we could also hear the wailing scream of sirens as other police cars and an ambulance raced to the spot.

I shuddered.

"I don't like to hear those sirens!" I exclaimed. "They always forebode trouble or heartache for someone, and they make me feel queasy in the stomach!"

Phil took my arm and tucked it in his.

"I know how you feel, my dear," he spoke sympathetically. "The way these sirens wail always makes me think of them as heralds of doom. However, we can be glad that on this occasion at least, we will not be concerned with this particular fanfare!"

He smiled down at me and squeezed my arm, and I summoned a smile in response as we retreated from the scene, to find another bridge which would take us over the river and back to our hotel.

Chapter Three

The large reception hall of the Mahler was bustling with people as we entered it, and the noise from the hotchpotch of European tongues which greeted our ears was like a cacophonous symphony created by a computer which had gone mad.

We crossed to the desk to obtain the keys for our rooms, and as we did so, I caught sight of Senga and Mabel. They spotted me at the same time and came hurrying over to speak to me, ogling Phil with great interest as they approached.

I introduced him to them, and then he took his leave, making no mention of getting in touch with me again, although the morning had gone so well that I felt sure he would.

"Isn't that the young man who rescued you from Ivy last night?" asked Senga, looking after him as he walked towards the elevators. "I must say I approve of your taste!"

I smiled. "I find him very pleasant!"

"I don't remember seeing him at previous conferences," frowned Mabel, "and he is not the kind of man I would miss seeing! What does he write?"

"He isn't with our conference," I explained. "He knows members of the other conference which is taking place here, and is here on business."

"At least he will protect you from Ivy," said Senga. "I don't see him standing nonsense from her, if she tries to hang around you!"

"Have you made any plans for lunch?" asked Mabel. "If not, why not join us in the Hayden Buffet? It is through the arcade, on the far side of the hall, and a few yards to the right. We'll keep a seat for you, if you want to go up to your room to freshen up first."

"I'll go up to my room later." I fell into step beside them, and they asked me what I had been doing with myself that morning as we made our way to the café.

They themselves had spent the morning with delegates from some of the other countries, whom they had met at previous meetings, and as we ate our lunch, which because of our expenses we limited to a plate of gulyas and a cup of coffee, they gave me quick pen pictures of some of the people I would be meeting that week. They also pointed out to me several foreign writing celebrities who, like ourselves, were enjoying a snack prior to the opening seminar of the conference which was to take place at two-thirty.

"I see from the program that Ivy is to be one of today's speakers," I remarked.

"Yes. She is popular with our Austrian hosts because of her sympathetic treatment of the Mayerling affair, which she used in her last year's best-seller," Senga told me. "Also, to give her her due, she is a witty and amusing speaker. She plays up to her audience, and they love it!"

"Maurizio Lenno is also speaking, and he can be equally amusing, and then there's Arnold Weissman," Mabel grimaced. "The discussions afterwards should be very interesting," she went on, and we reverted to talking shop.

"Here comes Dorinda!" Senga interrupted the conversation. "She is on her own, which means she has managed to dodge Ivy too, for a wonder!"

She signaled to a small, plump woman who

was standing in the doorway, peering anxiously into the restaurant, to come and join us.

"Dorinda Grey writes serious historical biographies as opposed to Ivy's fictitious ones," said Senga. "She always gets a good write-up from the critics, and there has always been a bit of rivalry between the two of them, the more so, I suppose, because they know each other quite well. They live quite near each other, they were at college together, and I think I am right in saying that she was actually one of the witnesses at Ivy's wartime wedding."

I listened with interest.

"She would know Ivy's husband, then?" I said, wondering why Ivy hadn't telephoned her instead of me during the night, since the woman to whom I was now being introduced would have been able to back her if her identification of Jan Sikorski had been correct.

I hadn't mentioned my middle-of-the-night conversation to either Senga or Mabel, because they had already told me how silly I had been allowing myself to be trapped by her for such a long time at the reception in the Palais Palffy. I did not want to see them raise their eyebrows in an "I told you so!" expression when they heard how Ivy had abused her knowledge of my room number by getting in touch with me in the small hours of the morning.

At the same time, curiosity prompted me, when the occasion presented itself, to ask Dorinda what Jan Sikorski looked like.

"In Ivy's eyes he was a god!" she smiled. "The tallest, handsomest and most brilliant man who

28

ever lived. In actual fact, he was quite ordinary in appearance, although his Polish Air Officer's uniform gave him a certain air of glamor.

"In fairness, I must say that he had a brilliant mind and was very quick-witted, so it was reasonable to assume that he was a graduate of Warsaw University."

"What was he like as a person?"

"I didn't like him. If Ivy hadn't had her head in her romantic clouds, she would have realized that he married her because he thought her father must be a rich man to own the rambling old vicarage where they lived, and because he had been able to afford to send Ivy to University. And of course, Ivy was always boasting that she was related to Lord somebody or other. I don't know which of them had the luckier escape when he was killed in the raid on Berlin!"

Mabel glanced at her watch.

"I must have a word with Paolo Verde," she mentioned the name of an Italian delegate, "and I want to make a few notes before the seminar starts." She pushed back her chair and rose to her feet.

"And I want to buy some postcards and post them off as soon as possible, or I shall arrive back home before them," said Senga.

"That's an idea," I agreed. "I noticed a shop in the Arcade had some attractive ones, and also a guidebook I would like to buy."

We went our various ways, to meet up again in the congress room, at whose entrance we were given earphones and receiver sets which we could tune in to French or German or English simultaneous translations of the speeches that would be made.

The platform party arrived. I recognized the president of the Austrian club, and the international secretary, Marguerite Dupont, who was chairing this particular meeting. Senga pointed out which of the other two men on the dais was Maurizio Lenno, and which Arnold Weissman, and we all stared with a frown of surprise at the vacant chair, where Ivy Sikorska should be sitting, but of Ivy there was still no sign.

The time to open the meeting arrived, and still Ivy had not turned up. The chairman looked at the president and there was a hurried confab, after which the senior British delegate was asked to go to reception and have Mrs. Sikorska paged.

Another ten minutes passed, and when Ivy still had not put in an appearance, after another hasty consultation Dorinda Grey was asked to deputize for her, and the meeting eventually got under way.

After the introductory speech for Arnold Weissman, I slipped quietly from the hall. Although Ivy meant nothing to me, and I did not even like what little I knew of her very much, I could not help worrying about the woman. Moreover, I felt I had some responsibility for her, since it was me she had taken into her confidence the night before and turned to for advice. After all, she was a stranger in a strange land, and she might even be lying ill in her bed with no one worrying about her, except insofar as she had delayed proceedings at the seminar!

Ivy's room was on the floor below mine, and as I hurried along the corridor towards it, I passed the blond young man who had been ogling me in the cocktail bar the previous evening.

He smiled and bowed to me and wished me "*Guten Tag.*" I politely returned his greeting, noting as I did so that he was wearing a name tag on his lapel which identified him as a member of the International Scientific Congress which was also in conference at the Mahler this week.

As I stopped outside Ivy's bedroom door, I noticed that the man had stopped at the end of the corridor and was looking back at me, as if watching to find out what room I occupied.

I smiled to myself. Serve him right if he checked the door after I was gone and dialed its number on the interroom service, only to get in touch with Ivy!

I raised my hand to knock at the door, but stopped it in mid-air as I spotted the "Do not disturb" notice which was hanging on the handle.

That was strange, I frowned. Surely Ivy wasn't still sleeping off her last night's hangover! If that was the case, it was time I wakened her, so I knocked loudly and waited for her call.

There wasn't a sound from the room, so I knocked again, but there was still no reply.

I shrugged. It was quite probable that Ivy was not in her room, and had forgotten, as I had forgotten on occasion, to remove the tag on leaving.

I knocked, half-hesitantly, a third time, and

waited another couple of seconds before returning to the elevator and going down to the first floor, where the conference rooms were situated.

There were several groups of people standing chatting in the broad passageway which led to the room I was making for. Most of them were delegates from one or the other of the meetings, and one or two of them I recognized as having met at the reception the previous evening. I was hurrying past Baron von Drachenberg and his wife when I heard a familiar voice.

I turned around and saw Phil Hunter standing near the doorway of the other conference hall, talking to an elderly, grey-haired man and an exceptionally lovely, tall young woman with long, gleaming chestnut hair and the fine, delicate, cream-colored skin that invariably goes with this hair coloring.

The cut of the bottle-green velvet suit she was wearing was Parisian, and the high-heeled shoes on her long slim feet looked as if they too were expensive.

As I was watching her with feminine curiosity, she put out her hand and caught at Phil's arm, smiling up at him with an air of intimacy as she said in a clear, carrying voice:

"Phil, darling, I did appreciate your coming to the airport to meet me today, especially after the shock you must have had when you learned I was coming to Vienna!"

She turned to the older man. "What did he look like when you broke the news of my impending visit to him, pleased or otherwise?" She cast another teasing glance at Phil.

"I was surprised to learn you were going to be here on business at the same time as your father and I," Phil smiled at her.

"But you are pleased our visits coincided?" she wheedled.

"What do you expect me to say to that, Sula?" Phil's tone held the same teasing note he had used in conversation with me earlier that day, and for no good reason I felt myself grow hot and cold with annoyance and hurt as I moved out of earshot.

I could not understand the annoyance, but I could understand feeling deflated. Phil Hunter had sought me out at the reception last night, and manipulated an introduction. He had telephoned me first thing this morning, indicating that he wanted to continue the acquaintanceship, and as the morning hours went by I had found myself growing attracted to Phil, enjoying his company in spite of our short acquaintanceship. I had even persuaded myself that he rather liked me too!

I had been looking forward to the development of our friendship during my week in Vienna. Now, with the unexpected arrival of the very attractive Sula, it was very doubtful if he would bother to get in touch with me again, even if he felt he ought to out of courtesy. Somehow I did not think Sula would approve of her young man spending any of his time with another woman. If I were in her shoes, I would certainly object strongly!

I was about to enter the conference hall when I bumped into Mabel, who was coming out. She grabbed my arm and directed me back into the corridor.

"Unless you want to be bored stiff, I would skip Dorinda's talk if I were you!" she advised me. "She is the sweetest person, and I am very fond of her, but as a speaker she is hopeless and rambles on and on. Senga is staying on out of goodness of heart, but Dorinda, on top of Arnold's dull performance, is too much for me to take!

"Come on," she urged me. "Let's go to the café in the hotel arcade and sample some of the luscious Austrian cakes. I noticed they had the most gorgeous Apfelstrudel when I passed this morning."

"You don't give me much option!" I laughed. "I must say I prefer Apfelstrudel to a boring speaker any day!"

The café was crowded, but we were fortunate to find a vacant table in a corner, and we made a beeline for it. I sat with my back to the room, and so it was Mabel who spotted Phil and his friends sitting at a table nearby.

"I say!" she remarked. "Your friend of this morning is sitting over at the window table with a most lovely redhead. I don't suppose it is his sister?" she pried, with the faintest note of malice in her voice.

"I wouldn't know," I shrugged, and switched my attention to the trolley of cakes which a waitress had wheeled towards us.

"Is it permitted?" asked a deep, foreign voice. "May I sit beside you?"

I looked up in surprise to see the fair man who

had seemed to be dogging me looking down at me.

"Yes! Yes! Do sit down," flustered Mabel. "These seats are not taken."

He sat down, and Mabel, who had been peering inquisitively at the name on his lapel, said, "I see you are attending the Science Conference here. We are with International Novelists."

"So?" he smiled. "Like me, are you missing a lecture in favor of coffee?"

"In favor of Apfelstrudel." I left Mabel to do the talking.

"For myself, I prefer the Sachertorte." He indicated his selection to the waitress, and as she carefully placed a large wedge of cake on his plate, he boldly leaned forward towards me so that he could read my name on the official badge which was pinned to my dress.

"Miranda Ogilvie," he read it slowly aloud. "Miranda is a name I recognize from your Shakespeare's *Tempest*, but Ogilvie," he enunciated my surname carefully, "that is a Scottish name, yes? The cousin of your queen is married to a man called Ogilvie, am I not right?"

I nodded, saying impishly as I did so, "Unfortunately, I am not related to that Ogilvie."

"No?" The young man's expression was quite serious. "I felt sure you were related to nobility. You have the air!"

I managed to stifle a giggle at his heavy-handed flattery, but I did not dare to catch Mabel's eye as he turned his attention to her.

"And you are, let me see," he bent forward to read the name she had pinned to her handbag.

"You are Mabel." He pronounced the word "Ma belle," "Mabel Angus, from England!"

"Where do you come from, Mr. Lippe?" asked Mabel. "You know, you are cheating by not putting the name of your country on your badge!"

He looked puzzled as he repeated the word with some difficulty.

"Chee-ting? What does that mean? Is it something not right?"

"No, no!" replied Mabel hastily. "I was merely wondering why you do not put your nationality beside your name as our conference members do."

"Now I understand," he nodded. "I do not have much occasion to speak your language, and some words I do not know. I am from East Germany," he informed us.

"Lippe?" I repeated his name. "Your minister of culture is called Frau Lippe. I don't suppose she is a relative?"

"But she is!" he said proudly. "I am her son!"

Our conversation was interrupted by the arrival of a red-faced Dorinda Grey, who was followed by Senga. Dorinda subsided into the one free chair at our table with a sigh of relief.

"Thank goodness that's over!" She smiled vaguely around the table. "I hate speechifying! Wait until I get hold of Ivy and give her a bit of my mind for letting me in for that ordeal!"

"Hasn't she turned up yet?" I asked.

Dorinda shook her head. "I don't understand it. I have been her friend for almost sixty years, and although she has done some silly things in that time I have never known her to act like this before. If she was feeling ill, I am sure I am the first person she would have contacted."

"I went along to her room just now and knocked on the door several times, but I got no reply. There was a 'Do not disturb' notice hanging on the handle, but I am sure she would have come to the door had she been in."

"How odd!" frowned Dorinda. "You are sure she wasn't in her room? Not that it is up to you to worry about her. You've known her less than twenty-four hours, after all, but I feel I ought to do something."

She glanced over her shoulder. "Where has the waitress got to? I must have a cup of strong black coffee to revive me after that speech of mine, and then I'll check up on Ivy."

She now cocked an interested eye at Karl Lippe, who was forking his cake into his mouth as fast as he could.

"Haven't we met before?" she asked him.

"Mr. Lippe was beside us in the cocktail bar last night," said Mabel. "He is with the other conference."

"I was sure I knew your face," Dorinda said smugly. "I pride myself on my memory for them."

Karl Lippe cleared his throat, pushed back his chair and stood up.

"I am intruding here, I think," he bowed politely. "Please excuse me."

"Oh! Do stay!" invited Mabel, but he shook his head.

"Thank you, no. In any case, I see friends of mine signaling to me to join them, so I go, but," he looked at me although he addressed his remarks to us all, "I hope to see you all at the joint reception for our two delegations, which the Bürgermeister is giving at the Rathaus tonight."

Lippe shook hands with each one of us in turn, and held my fingers lingeringly as he said in his serious voice:

"I am so glad that you are not related to the nobility, Fräulein Ogilvie!"

He went hurrying off to join two elderly men who were pacing up and down on the pavement outside like prison guards.

Senga watched him go.

"Even if that man doesn't believe in the nobility and class distinctions and the like," she grinned at me, "I wouldn't hold it against him! It is obvious that he finds you to his liking, Miranda. In fact," she looked across at her friend, "Mabel and I were remarking how he has been ogling you since last night, so I think you should be nice to him. We all have to do our bit, you know, to improve East-West relations!"

I laughed and said nothing, but I had already decided to be nice to Lippe, as Senga was suggesting.

I had noticed Phil Hunter cast an occasional interested look at our table when Karl had joined us. If I encouraged Lippe, it would be one way of showing Phil that I would not be sitting around waiting for him to date me on the odd occasion when Sula had plans which did not include him.

Chapter Four

Dorinda Grey swallowed the last drop of her coffee, and reluctantly decided that she ought to find out if Ivy was in her room before the afternoon session of talks and discussions resumed after the coffee break.

"I do hope she is in her room," she remarked as she stood up. "If she is, I shall drag her down so that she can take over from me at question time. She is so much better than I at that sort of thing."

"We'll see you in the conference room, Dorinda." Senga glanced at her watch. "You will have to hurry, you know. There's only another five minutes before the session resumes."

Phil Hunter, who was following his friends from the café, stopped to ask me how the meeting was going.

"Ivy Sikorska didn't turn up to make her speech!" I told him. "Her absence caused quite a stir!"

"Maybe she hasn't recovered from last night!" he smiled down at me. "You had better keep an eye on her tonight, Miranda, and ration the number of glasses she accepts from the waiters! I suppose you will be going to the Rathaus tonight?" he added.

"Our very serious-minded young scientist from East Germany will be very disappointed if Miranda doesn't put in an appearance!" said Mabel wickedly.

Phil's eyebrows raised fractionally.

"Yes, I saw young Lippe talking to you," he looked at me, "and I wasn't at all surprised when Major Dietrich signaled to him to come to heel. Our East German friends are not very keen on their men hobnobbing with pretty western girls for any length of time, so be careful, Miranda," he adjured me with a twinkle in his eyes. "You might become the cause of an International Incident!"

He hurried off to rejoin his friends before I could think up a suitable reply, and as he caught up with them, I saw the girl turn around for a moment to take another look at me before she moved through the doorway.

"We had better get along to the conference room," suggested Senga. "It wouldn't look good if half the British representatives didn't put in an appearance this afternoon, especially after the way Ivy failed to turn up."

The final speaker of the day was Maurizio Lenno, an Italian writer and journalist and a friend of Mabel's, who gave a witty and amusing speech about trying to reconcile fact and fiction in the historical novel. After the applause for his talk died away, a general discussion on what the three speakers had said was opened, and some lively exchanges followed.

Surprisingly, Dorinda had not returned to take part in the argument, or to answer questions in regard to her own speech, and it was plain from the expressions on the faces of the platform party as they glanced at us, that they were annoyed at the casual attitude of our representatives.

A few minutes before the meeting was due to be wound up, however, Dorinda, looking very pale and distraught, appeared in the doorway and made her way to the platform. Sitting down on a vacant chair, she whispered a few words to the chairman.

Marguerite Dupont gasped at what she had been told, and looked at Dorinda with a startled expression, as if she didn't believe her. Dorinda confirmed what she had said with a grave nod, whereupon Madame Dupont rapped on the table for silence.

When she had got everyone's attention, she said slowly, in English, "I have just had a most distressing piece of news, ladies and gentlemen. Mrs. Ivy Sikorska, the English delegate who was to have addressed us earlier this afternoon, is dead!"

A bewildered hush followed her words, before a babel of excited voices swept through the hall.

What had happened? Had there been an accident? When had she died? The questions came from all sides.

Again Madame Dupont rapped for silence.

"I understand Mrs. Sikorska died in her sleep early this morning," she replied.

She then turned to the other members of the platform party, as if invoking their backing of her next words.

"I think, in view of this tragedy, we should bring the present meeting to a close."

"What about the reception in the Rathaus this evening?" called someone.

"There will be no changes in the arrangements as far as it is concerned," she replied slowly. "We shall meet, as scheduled, in the foyer of the hotel at eight-fifteen, when we shall be taken by autobus to the Rathaus."

"I can't believe it!" Mabel gaped at Senga and me. "I just can't believe it! Ivy seemed so indestructible, somehow!"

She rose to her feet. "Let's get hold of Dorinda and find out exactly what happened."

We struggled past the other members of the audience to reach an ashen-faced Dorinda, but she could tell us no more than she had told Madame Dupont.

She had gone up to Ivy's room, and when she did not get a reply to her persistent knocking, she had summoned a chambermaid to open the door. They had entered the room together and found Ivy lying on top of the bed, still dressed in the black lace evening gown she had worn to the Palais Palffy.

From the way she was lying and the way her open eyes gazed sightlessly at the ceiling, they did not need the confirmation of the doctor, who was later summoned by the manager, to tell them she was dead and had been dead for almost fifteen hours.

"With usual medical caution, he said he could not give a cause of death until he had examined the body, but I think she had had a heart attack."

I felt a pang of guilt. Perhaps if I had gone

along to see Ivy in response to her excited phone call, I would have been in the room with her when she took ill, and might have been able to summon help.

However, Dorinda's next words salved my conscience.

"Poor Ivy!" she sniffed. "I didn't realize she was feeling ill when she telephoned me last night, or rather early this morning. It was about two o'clock and I had just got back from a private party given by Madame Dupont, when the buzzer went. I picked up the receiver and it was Ivy. She said she had been trying to get in touch with me for ages, and she wanted me to go along to her room.

"I was asking her what was so urgent when she told me to hang on, she thought she had heard a knock on her door. After a few seconds she returned to the phone and told me she was sorry she had troubled me, that everything was fine now, and she gave a silly giggle."

Dorinda sniffed once more. "I thought she was a bit tiddly, from the excited way she was speaking, and the way she simply dropped the receiver on the cradle to cut me off. She probably didn't realize how ill she was."

We were all very subdued as we left the hall, and Senga sensibly suggested that we ought to go for a walk in the fresh air, instead of sitting mournfully in the lounge talking about poor Ivy.

I felt the better for the brisk stroll along the Wollzeile to the Graben. Although the air was cold and a fine drizzle was falling, the wind had dropped, and it was pleasant to feel fresh air and dewy dampness on my cheeks after the near-hothouse temperature of the big modern hotel.

I found myself looking at the tastefully decorated shop windows along the way with interest, and then felt annoyed with myself, because I was not as upset by Ivy's death as I felt I should be. Dorinda's announcement had shocked me momentarily, and I had also had a momentary pang of conscience, remembering my last abrupt words to her, but in fact, Ivy had been a stranger to me; someone I had met, and not particularly liked, for a few hours the previous day. It was only reasonable that I was not deeply affected by her passing.

I felt another twinge of remorse as I stood in front of the long mirror in my bedroom later that evening, studying my reflection and hoping that the demurely high-necked, long-sleeved, kimono-style dress of hyacinth blue silk (a color which exactly matched my eyes) would attract Phil Hunter's admiring attention.

It was heartless of me to feel so lighthearted, so much looking forward to the social evening in Vienna's magnificent new Rathaus, when poor Ivy Sikorska, who would have thoroughly enjoyed such an evening, was dead. Yet try as I might I could not control the bubbling excitement in my veins as I fastened the two narrow gold clasps which kept my sleekly brushed, slightly curling hair neatly pinned back from my temples.

I added a touch of the expensive Dior perfume I had bought in the duty-free shop at London Airport to my throat, behind my ears, and to the pulses on my wrists, slung the mink jacket I had borrowed from my mother over my shoulders, and went down to the reception hall to join Mabel Angus and my other new friends.

Phil Hunter, his friend Sula, and her father were standing talking to Mabel as I emerged from the elevator, and womanlike, as I walked towards them I shot an interested look at Phil's friend.

She was wearing an ankle-length coat of white fox furs, and her hair was piled on top of her head in a Burmese bun which was skewered into position with a sparkling diamanté comb. She looked beautiful and exotic, and some of the euphoria I had experienced, looking at myself in the bedroom mirror and feeling pleased with my own choice of gown, vanished as I looked at her. Compared with Sula, I was like a suburban housewife in the presence of the empress of Persia!

Phil saw me and smiled at me.

"Your friends tell me that they don't mind if we join your party, Miranda. Sir Jack says he has had enough of his fellow physicists for one day!"

He then introduced me to Sir Jack Neilson and his daughter, and Sula studied me, as the introductions were made, with as much interest as I had accorded her.

As we stood waiting for the arrival of the buses which were to take us to the Rathaus, I gazed around the hall, and at the far end I spotted Karl Lippe and the two men he had been talking to earlier in the afternoon. They were standing with a group of people, including a small, plump girl in a severely tailored black skirt and blouse, and two older women, one tall and attractive looking, the other, like the girl, small and sturdy of physique.

Karl was looking in our direction, a sullen expression on his squarely handsome face, and Phil Hunter turned to me and observed with a mischievous smile, "I don't think young Lippe is going to be allowed to talk to you tonight, Miranda. He blotted his copybook by spending so much time with you in the café this afternoon, and now Major Dietrich is going to make him toe the party line!"

"Where's Dorinda?" I turned to Mabel, ignoring Phil's teasing.

"Dorinda isn't coming with us tonight," she shook her head. "Ivy's death, and the fact that she was the one to find her, has shocked her deeply. After all," she added, "in spite of their frequent quarrels and arguments, their friendship, if you could call their relationship by that name, spanned almost sixty years, and she is bound to feel a sense of loss."

"I was sorry to hear about Mrs. Sikorska's death," Phil spoke seriously now. "I met her only briefly last night, but she struck me as a woman with a very strong personality."

The doorkeeper announced that our buses had arrived, so we filed out to take our places in them.

Sula Neilson edged into the seat beside me, saying with a smile, "You are so nice and slim, Miranda, that we shan't get our dresses crumpled up as we would if we sat beside Father or Phil."

I soon found that this wasn't her only reason for sitting beside me, for as the bus moved off, she asked casually, "Have you known Phil long?"

"Why, no!" I was surprised at the question. "I met him last night for the first time."

"Oh!" she breathed thoughtfully. "I thought you were old friends, from the way he spoke of you, but I must have picked him up wrongly." She glanced over at Phil, who was sitting diagonally across the passage from us, alongside her father.

I wondered what Phil had said to her, to give her the impression we weren't new acquaintances, but I did not want to betray too great an interest in him by asking her, so instead I said, "You have a most unusual forename. I have never known anyone called Sula. Is it of foreign origin?"

She laughed. "It is a hotchpotch of a name, but it always makes an interesting subject of conversation when I meet people for the first time, and helps to break the ice!

"You see," she went on to explain, "my mother loves flowers, as her mother did before her, and the girls in my grandmother's family were all called flower names. I have an Aunt Lily, an Aunt Rose, and an Aunt Violet, and my mother's name is Marigold!" she looked at me, smiling. "When I tell you that my mother's maiden name was Garden, you can imagine some of the comments that were made about her!"

I chuckled with amusement, and Phil looked around.

"What is amusing you two girls?" he asked curiously. "Can we share the joke?"

"I was telling Miranda about the Garden flower girls!" smiled Sula and turned her attention back to me.

"Mother wanted to call me a flower name too," she continued, "but Father put his foot down very firmly! In the end, as in all good marriages, they compromised. I was christened Susan Lala, shortened to Sula."

"Where does the compromise come in?" I was puzzled.

"That's simple. Susan, if you look up the meaning of the name, is a lily, and Lala is a tulip! Sula is a much more interesting name than Lily Tulip, now, isn't it?"

I laughed again. In spite of my earlier quite unwarranted feeling of jealousy for the young woman sitting beside me, I was growing to like her. Apart from her air of elegance and chic she was witty and amusing, a combination of virtues which would attract any man, and particularly, I thought, a man like Phil Hunter. Beside her I must appear very ordinary, and it was a wonder he had spared me a second look.

The bus stopped outside the Rathaus, and as we got out Phil took Sula by the arm, while her father courteously acted as my escort into the building.

I had thought the Palais Palffy a magnificent example of the Viennese style of architecture, but the new Town Hall was equally magnificent, with its great staircase and marble pillars, and massive crystal chandeliers hanging from the ceilings reflecting the lights like a conglomeration of sparkling stars.

After being received by the mayor in the main salon, the delegates made their way into various anterooms, where tables were laid out for supper.

Sir Jack Neilson, who had attended similar functions here before, led us to a table in the corner of the main room, where we could see all that went on.

To my surprise, our party, which also included Arnold Weissman and Maurizio Lenno, who were partnering Senga and Mabel, was joined (to Sir Jack's tactfully concealed annoyance) by Karl Lippe and his friends, the two men he had been with that afternoon and the three women I had seen with them in the Mahler a short time ago.

The older men looked as if they had been cast in the same mould. They were both of average height, inclined to portliness, with receding hairlines, and they both sported greying Franz Josef-style whiskers and sideburns.

The more aggressive-mannered of the two men was introduced as Major Dietrich, whose name Phil had already mentioned to me, and I was taken aback to learn that the shyer man with the square-shaped dark glasses was Karl's father, Helmut Lippe, whose name even I recognized as that of a man who was doing important work in the field of nuclear physics. The three women had unpronounceable names, which I made no effort to learn since they made no friendly overtures either to me or anyone else in our party, although they eyed Sula and myself with frowning interest.

In fact, only Karl and Major Dietrich made any attempt at conversation with us, which made me decide that it was possible that none of the others either spoke or understood English.

The food served by an army of elderly waiters was magnificent, and Viennese hospitality saw to it that wine flowed without stint. Karl drank glass after glass, with no apparent enjoyment of the bouquet, as he sat facing me across the table. He rarely took his eyes off me, although he seldom addressed me, and I grew embarrassed each time I looked up and caught him staring at me.

I was also aware that Major Dietrich was eyeing me covertly from time to time, and I resented his interest.

Sir Jack politely essayed a conversation with his fellow physicists but his efforts fell flat, and all six of them seemed more interested in the food they were served than in trying to overcome the barriers of nationality. Even Karl, who had been so talkative in the afternoon, was as silent as the others.

"I wonder why they came to sit with us instead of sitting at a table by themselves," whispered Mabel to me. "I feel as though I am sitting opposite a selection of wax dummies!"

In the background, an orchestra was playing the inevitable selection of Strauss waltzes, and when we had finished eating there was an announcement over the loudspeaker system that tables would be cleared from the center of the main salon, so that those who wished to dance could do so.

The announcement galvanized Karl into action. He pushed back his chair, stood up, and looking across the table at me he said in his slow, careful English, "May I dance with you, Fräulein Ogilvie?"

I could not refuse his request, although he must have been as aware as I was that his proposal did not please his fellow countrymen—and in particular, displeased the three women.

Karl's manner of dancing was as stiff as his personality. He held me at arm's length as we circled the floor a number of times. While we gyrated around and around, I noticed that Phil and Sir Jack were gallantly dancing with two of the East German women, and that Sula was being stoically propelled around the floor by Major Dietrich, who seemed determined to keep within earshot of Karl and myself.

When the music stopped we returned to the table, but no sooner had we sat down than Major Dietrich was on his feet again, asking us to excuse him and his party because they had to leave now. There was a committee meeting they had to attend.

Karl gave him a resentful look, and for a moment I thought he was going to stay with us, for he remained seated.

Sensing his rebellious attitude, I noted how Dietrich's lips tightened into a thin line of annoyance, and an angry expression came into his eyes. He was about to say something when the elder Lippe touched his son's shoulder and said softly:

"Come, Karl!"

The moment of revolt was quashed. Karl, still unsmiling, rose reluctantly to his feet, and with a jerky bow he bade us all good night before trailing after the others from the salon.

"I wouldn't encourage the attentions of that young man if I were you, Miss Ogilvie," Sir Jack turned to me. "You may find the situation amusing, my dear, but I am afraid young Lippe's interest in you does not meet with official approval! The East German Republic would not want one of its up and coming geniuses in spacecraft technology to defect to the West for the love of a pretty young woman!"

I was too taken up with the group who were leaving to pay much attention to his remarks, and I bit my lip in perplexity as I watched them.

"What's wrong, Miranda?" asked Phil. "Are you put out because party loyalty takes precedence over personal choice?"

"No! No! It's not that!" I shook my head. "It was just that for a moment, something that was said or done a moment ago reminded me of something," I gave a shamefaced smile, "and I can't think what, or why it seems important that I should remember.

"That might sound ridiculous to you, but surely you also have had a similar experience of twanging on the string of memory, without making the music of recall! It's most aggravating!"

"And probably quite unimportant!" laughed

Sula, turning to Phil and laying her fingers on his sleeve. "Listen!" she said to him. "They are playing our tune. We simply must dance to it again!"

The pair of them went off to the dance floor hand in hand to the strains of "Windmills of Your Mind," but I was scarcely conscious of their going as I sat, staring blankly at the vase of scarlet carnations on our table, trying to recall what it was that had stimulated the fleeting moment of recollection.

However, I soon forgot the problem, for now that Karl and his friends were no longer with us to act as a damper on our spirits, our party livened up.

Arnold Weissman, the American delegate, had been a dull orator, but he was a witty after-dinner companion, and in between dances he kept us amused by telling us stories of some of the famous people he had met when he had worked for a time as a TV announcer. As a matter of fact, he had worked at so many different jobs that I asked him when he found time to write!

He grinned and told me that he didn't actually do any writing, but taped all his stories when he lay in bed and let a stenographer do the dull work of putting them on paper!

I danced with Arnold and with Maurizio and with Sir Jack, but I enjoyed dancing with Phil most of all. Our steps seemed to fit perfectly, and I experienced a thrill of physical pleasure each time he took me in his arms and we danced together to the haunting music of the Viennese violins and the Viennese zither.

Even when the reception came to an end and we had to leave the Rathaus, we were all still in a happy mood, and we linked arms in line as we strolled across the Rathausplatz to the Burgtheater.

The early evening drizzle had ceased. The moon had come out from behind the rain clouds and shone over the city, giving its rooftops and spires an air of fairytale beauty.

Even though I was not alone with Phil Hunter on this pleasant night, at least we were walking arm in arm, close together, and he seemed to be paying as much attention to me as he was to Sula, who was clinging to his other arm.

I felt light-headed, lighthearted and content, with never a thought of poor Ivy Sikorska, and, fortunately, never a suspicion of what her crossing of my path was going to mean to me!

Chapter Five

I slept late the following morning. I had forgotten to set my alarm before getting into bed, and it was a firm knocking on the door of my room which finally wakened me.

A quick glance at my watch told me it was nine o'clock, the time I had ordered breakfast to be brought to me, and I realized it must be the floor waiter who was knocking.

I swung out of bed, grabbed hold of my quilted housecoat and struggled into it as I hurried across the room to open the door.

As usual, he set down the tray on the table beside the window, and once he had gone I pulled back the curtains and slid aside one of the windows to let in a breath of the crisp, cold morning air.

I stretched my arms out lazily as I looked over the city. It was going to be a lovely day. The sun was shining from a cloudless blue sky and silvery white frost sparkled on the rooftops over which the inevitable black crows flew in their endless circles, croaking out their mournful dirges.

A string of coaches, roofs covered with a blanket of snow, came into view on the snaking railway line far below me, and as it disappeared into a tunnel I turned from the window and went over to switch on the radio incorporated in the table by my bedside.

Although my German was a trifle rusty from lack of practice, I was able to make out from the weather forecast that there had been heavy falls of snow in Eastern Europe and over the Swiss Alps. Winter had come early to Central Europe this year, although the announcer went on to add that the snows might not reach the Vienna area for another day or so.

I switched off the radio, showered and dressed, and sat down to enjoy a leisurely breakfast while studying the conference agenda for the day. There was to be a seminar in the morning, but after midday, we were free until evening.

The reception hall was crowded as usual when I arrived there to meet Senga and Mabel as arranged the previous evening. There was a lot of coming and going, with new arrivals crowding the desk, and other people checking out. Groups of delegates from the two conferences stood chatting together before starting the business of the day. It was a repeat of the scene I had witnessed here yesterday morning. There was no sign of added excitement. Ivy Sikorska's death had not added a single ripple to the smooth waters of hotel management, and to my surprise, not even Senga or Mabel mentioned it as we gossiped of the events at the reception the previous evening.

It was not until I asked them where Dorinda was that a reference was made to the dead woman.

"Dorinda is not going to come to the seminar," Mabel told me. "She got in touch with me to tell me so. It seems that she was Ivy's executrix and so she has been roped in by the authorities to attend to matters concerning her death."

"What a shame!" said Senga. "That means she is bound to miss quite a few meetings, surely?"

"She is going to join us for lunch, and she also hopes to come with us to St. Stephen's in the afternoon," said Mabel. "You will come with us too, won't you, Miranda?"

"I am sorry," I excused myself. "I have been invited for lunch and to spend the afternoon with the family I stayed with during my student days in Vienna, and they are asking some of the other young people I met then to come and meet me again."

I spent a very pleasant afternoon with the Bohnenkamps. We talked nonstop about old friends, and the fun we used to have, and places we had visited that summer two years ago.

Time flew past very quickly. There was so much to say, and I was pleased to find that I hadn't forgotten as much German as I thought I had, although the occasional word still eluded me.

When a glance at my watch told me it was five o'clock, I could scarcely believe it, and had to ask hastily to be excused. That evening at seven o'clock there was to be a special show in the famous Spanish Riding School in the Hofburg, and since I had not been able to see the world-famous Lipizzaner horses on my first visit to Vienna, I did not want to miss this special opportunity of seeing them tonight.

Rudi Bohnenkamp drove me back to the hotel in his brand new white Porsche, and I was childishly delighted to be seen slipping out of it by Sula and Phil, who were standing chatting in the hotel entrance.

I saw Phil raise his thick eyebrows and a speculative look in Sula's green eyes as I waved to Rudi before walking towards them.

"You don't let the grass grow under your feet, do you?" observed Phil. "I didn't know any of your writing friends could afford a car like that!"

"Rudi is not a writer," I assured him. "He is an old friend, from the days when I was a student in Vienna for a few months."

"So by returning to Vienna, you are mixing business and pleasure?" he queried.

"Yes, I am!" I agreed lightly, deliberately not telling him that Rudi, like most of my other friends here, was now married and had a couple of children. "I was delighted when I learned that the conference was to be in Vienna this year, since it meant I could kill two birds with one stone, so to speak."

"Isn't it a shame about Dorinda Grey?" Sula edged her way into the conversation as she and Phil accompanied me into the reception hall.

"Why? What has Dorinda been doing?" I asked in astonishment.

"Weren't you with her when the accident happened?"

"What accident?" I gaped at them. "Oh, no! Don't tell me that something dreadful has happened to Dorinda now!"

"You would almost think there was a jinx on your delegation!" said Sula, as the clerk at the desk handed us our room keys. "I am not very sure of the details," she went on, "but we were told that a pile of wooden planking, which was to be used to help shore up the underground workings near St. Stephen's, collapsed on top of her as she was walking past, and she was rushed to the hospital."

"It is all right," put in Phil quickly, seeing my look of shock. "She is not as badly hurt as she might have been. She has a broken leg, and a badly bruised arm and shoulder, and a nasty gash above her temple, and will be kept in the hospital for a week or so, but she could easily have been killed."

"Poor Dorinda!" I sighed deeply. "This is not a conference she is going to forget in a hurry, what with her friend Ivy dying, and now this! Is she allowed any visitors?"

"Not for a couple of days, I have been told," said Sula. "She is also suffering from shock and concussion and the doctors insist she be kept quiet."

We entered the elevator together. Sula got out at the tenth floor, the floor on which Ivy Sikorska's room had been, and Phil got out at the eleventh floor with me.

His room was at the end of a different corridor from mine, but before we parted company he told me that he was meeting the Neilsons in the hotel cocktail bar, prior to going on to the special performance of the Spanish Riding School which had been arranged for all the international delegates by the Bundeswirtschaftskammer, and he asked if I would like to meet him there.

I looked at him curiously.

"You aren't a delegate, Phil, so how come you get in on all the special receptions and things?" I asked him.

"I told you before, Miranda. I have friends in high places!" he smiled.

"You also said that you were here in Vienna on business, but I can't say I have seen you do much work!" I retorted.

"All work and no play—you know the adage!" he twinkled, "but you haven't answered me,

Miranda." He looked at me. "Would you like to come with us this evening, or have you already made other arrangements?"

"Nothing definite was said," I replied slowly. "Mabel and Senga have been very kind including me in all their parties, and they insist I mustn't feel out of things since this is my first conference, but I don't like imposing on them all the time."

"Then that settles it!" said Phil decisively. "Tonight you will come with us, won't you?"

I nodded agreement, and we parted company.

I was excited at the thought of seeing the world-famous Lipizzaner horses in action. I had read about them, seen pictures of them, even sent picture postcards of them to my family and friends, but I had never seen the white horses in the flesh.

It was a bitterly cold evening, and although Sula was wearing a long, black woollen dress topped by a black fox fur coat, and I had put on a long skirt of my clan tartan with a cosy polo-neck sweater in dark green and a thick plaid, ankle-length cloak, Sir Jack insisted that instead of going with the other delegates by bus, tonight we would go by ourselves in a taxi to the Hofburg.

We arrived several minutes before the busloads and were shown to seats which faced down the long, rectangular building. I looked about me with great interest. The magnificent white baroque hall looked more like a splendid ballroom than a riding school, but it was as a winter riding school that it had been designed by von Erlach for Karl VI. As I studied it with admiration, counting sixteen Corinthian columns carrying the gallery in the main hall, and noting the shape of the ceiling and the deep insets of the windows, I wasn't surprised that it had taken several years to complete.

Tonight, in honor of the foreign guests who were attending the display, it was decked with greenery, and exotic hothouse blooms formed a bank of color in front of the place where we were sitting.

"I expect you saw the horses when you were in Vienna on your last visit?" Phil turned to me.

I shook my head.

"Unfortunately, no."

"Then you are in for a treat, Miranda. To me, no other exhibition of horsemanship measures up to this one. In fact, I think I am right in saying that it is the oldest and last riding school in the world in which the art of classical riding in its purest form is still carried on."

"The horses themselves are absolutely gorgeous!" said Sula. "I suppose you know that only horses of Spanish origin, Lipizzans, are used."

"Yes," I nodded. "I have read about them."

The hall was filled with people, and when they had settled, the orchestra began to play the tune "Festlicher Eintritt," and to its music a selection of four-year-old stallions, their coats still quite dark in color (for they don't turn white until they are seven or eight years old), came into the hall and were put through their paces, to prepare them for future, more intricate steps.

These young horses were followed by horses trained to the principles of classical horsemanship, and they went through difficult and intricate routines with a lightness and delicacy of movement that made their performance seem all too easy.

"These are the exercises which are required in the Olympic Games," Sir Jack whispered to me. "But somehow, when you see them performed here, they seem much more natural and effortless."

With each change of music, different horses came in and performed different steps and different routines, and I found the names of the animals as interesting and romantic as the setting in which they worked. Pluto Stornella, Favory Theodorosta, Conversano Basilica, Neapolitano Nautika—the names were magic-sounding.

The moment above all for which I had been waiting arrived, and I leaned forward in my seat when the most gifted horses, horses possessing great strength and intelligence, came forward to perform the breathtaking routine of "Schools Above the Ground."

First came the Levade, when the horses squat on their haunches and lift their forefeet off the ground, to maintain this position for some time. Next came the Courbette, when the horses execute several forward leaps on their hind quarters without touching the ground with their forefeet, and finally came the Capriole, when the horses leap simultaneously with all four feet, and at the height of the leap, with the body horizontal in the air, kick violently with their hind legs.

The audience clapped and cheered horses and riders, and they all seemed to enjoy the applause.

Even when the horses had their feet on the ground, because their hooves were polished the same tanny brown as the peat which covered the arena, they still seemed to be walking on air, for hooves and peat merged into one color, and the white legs of the stallions seemed to be moving in space!

The final quadrille, a ballet of white stallions performing difficult figures to the rhythm of the Polonaise, the Gavotte and finally to the stirring music of the *Prinz Eugen Marsch*, was an experience I knew I would not forget in a hurry.

I clapped and clapped at the team as they trotted out of sight, and Phil laughed at my enthusiasm.

"You know, Miranda," he teased me, "you don't need to express your delight by banging your hands together like that! Your appreciation shows in your eyes and the glow of your smile!"

"Miranda wouldn't be much good as a smuggler!" Sula looked at me with laughter in her eyes. "She has much too expressive a face! The excisemen would spot her guilt right away!"

As we made for the exit, Sula glanced at her watch.

"It is only nine o'clock," she said. "That's much too early to go back to the Mahler."

"I'm afraid I shall have to return there, my dear," her father said. "I have one or two notes I want to check over for my talk tomorrow morning."

"And I have some work to attend to as well," added Phil.

Sula pouted.

"Miranda and I can't very well wander about the streets on our own," she observed, "so we shall have to come with you. I am starving!" she moaned. "I have had nothing to eat except a plate of gulyas soup since breakfast, and I thought we would go somewhere for a meal before returning to the hotel."

"We can have a meal in the hotel before I go up to my room," proposed Sir Jack. "The prices in the Mahler are as reasonable as anywhere else."

"But it is so dull, seeing the same old faces!" protested Sula perversely. "I wanted to go to a Weinkeller and eat exotic Hungarian food and listen to some Schrammelmusik! Come on, Father!" she urged. "You can't fool me! You already know your speech by heart. You have taped it often enough!"

Her father smiled and looked at me.

"Do all daughters try to twist their fathers around their fingers?" he asked.

"This is the city of Freud and psychoanalysis," I smiled back at him, "so perhaps someone here will be able to answer your question for you— and give you a reason for their answer!"

Phil took Sula's arm.

"We shall listen to your Schrammelmusik another night," he told her firmly. "I'm not your father, and you can't twist me around your finger! I have to go back to the Mahler for a chat with Otto Memmling, and that's that! However," he added, "we will have time to take something to eat in the hotel before he arrives."

"I don't know why I like you, Phil!" pouted Sula. "You always bully me into doing things I don't want to do!"

Phil looked around for a taxi to take us back to the Mahler, but there were so many people with the same idea that after a time we gave up trying to flag one down and walked briskly towards the Graben, on past Stephansplatz, to the Wollzeile which led directly to the Mahler.

Mabel and Senga and their escorts had been fortunate enough to get hold of a taxi near the Hofburg, and they were already in the dining room as we entered and looked around for a vacant table.

As the head waiter led us past where they were sitting, Senga smiled at us and said, "One thing about Vienna, you can't say it lacks excitement! It is no wonder so many thrillers and spy stories get written about it! What do you think of the latest happening?"

We stopped to look at her.

"Why, what else has been happening?" asked Phil.

"Surely you have heard about it!" Mabel looked up at us in surprise. "The girl's murder made local headlines this morning and was mentioned on the local radio as well."

Phil gave me a frowning glance and unexpectedly took hold of my elbow in a firm grip.

"Are you talking about the girl whose body was found beneath the bridge over the Wienfluss, just across the road from here?"

I was startled by his words.

"Don't tell me this was the accident we took pains to avoid being involved in yesterday morning!"

He nodded. "I was hoping you hadn't read about it in the papers, Miranda. I thought it might upset you."

"Don't tell me you were there when the body was found!" gasped Senga, goggle-eyed. "What a shock you would have had if you had recognized her!"

"Why should we have recognized her?" demanded Phil, puzzled.

"It was just possible you might have seen her before," replied Senga. "She has been identified as Klara Fischer, who was a chambermaid in this hotel! She actually worked on the late shift on the tenth floor, and it is assumed that she was killed shortly after she came off duty."

"My bedroom is on the tenth floor!" Sula interrupted her with a gasp.

"So was Ivy's!"

I don't know what prompted me to make that remark, unless I felt that it was a coincidence that the two women should have died on the same night, but apart from Phil, who shot me a frowning glance, no one paid any attention to what I had said.

"The management of the hotel are not going to be too pleased about the publicity her death is bringing to the hotel," shrugged Mabel. "Even though she only worked here, I believe there have been several people wandering in to have a look around the floor where she was on duty!"

"I hope it wasn't the pretty little blonde who ogled me when I was going into my bedroom, after returning from the Palais Palffy!" put in Sir Jack. "She seemed very young, but she had a very 'come hither' look in her eyes!"

"Then I hope you have an alibi for that night, Sir Jack!" said Senga pertly. "As it happens Klara was young and small and blonde, and the night porter says she left the hotel not long after two o'clock, to join a man with grey hair who was waiting for her on the other side of the road. He didn't pay much attention to him, because he thought it was her father who had come to take her home, but the police now think that he was her killer."

"I think it is horrible!" I shuddered, and my enjoyment of the evening faded.

"Let's not talk about it any more!" said Phil firmly. "In any case, if we don't get a move on, we shall lose our table!"

Still holding my arm, he led me away from Senga's table, and we were followed by Sula and her father as we made for the spot at the far end of the dining room where the head waiter was standing impatiently with his hand on the back of the chair he had pulled out ready for me to sit down.

Although I had felt hungry when Sula had originally suggested we go for a meal, and the brisk walk back from the Hofburg in the sharp night air had added an edge to my appetite, after learning the details of what had happened to the little chambermaid in the Stadtpark, I found I was no longer interested in food. For some unaccountable reason, the death of a young girl I had never seen struck me as being more tragic, and weighed more heavily on my thoughts, than Ivy Sikorska's death.

My strange mood of depression was not helped by my awareness of the presence of Major Dietrich, who was sitting on a stool at the counter of the narrow cocktail bar which was on an elevated gallery that ran the length of the dining room and overlooked it.

Each time I happened to glance in his direction I had to look hurriedly away again, for he was staring directly at me with a steady, unblinking gaze that made me feel uneasy.

There was something about Dietrich's manner that frightened me, although I had no specific reason for my fear or the intense dislike I felt for him.

He made me think of a dedicated hunter. A man who liked to kill for the sake of killing. A man who would stalk his prey relentlessly until he had it in his sights, and then relish the terror of his victim as he deliberately squeezed the trigger!

Chapter Six

Two days later I was finishing breakfast and had switched on the radio to listen to the local station that gave the weather forecast for the region, when my telephone buzzed.

"Good morning, Miranda," said a cheerful

voice. "Phil Hunter here. How are you feeling this morning?"

"Phil!" I exclaimed. "How nice of you to phone! I was sorry I didn't go to Sula's party last night, but I was very tired."

"I thought you looked a bit under the weather when I left you. That is one of the reasons why I got in touch so early. You sound brighter, I must say!"

"A good night's sleep did the trick," I told him. "I was tired out with all the excitement of the past few days. I am not used to living in such a gay whirl!"

"You are a country girl at heart, is that it?" he joked. "You don't look the part!"

I smiled, amused at his chat.

"How did the party go, by the way?" I asked.

"The way these hotel room parties usually go," he replied lightly. "Everyone spoke too much, one or two drank too much, a few of us argued too much, and one or two overstayed their welcome and had to be firmly ejected. You .didn't miss much, in other words!" he assured me.

"Were Senga and Mabel there?"

"Yes. In point of fact, your cronies were much more amusing and less argumentative than Sir Jack's physicists, who take themselves very seriously. Arnold Weissman was particularly good company."

"Was Karl Lippe there with his friends?" I was curious to know. "Sula said she was going to ask them."

"When you told her that you wouldn't be

joining us, she decided not to. You appear to be the only one outside his own bloc young Lippe talks to, so his presence without you would have been a washout. Had you met him before?" he queried casually.

"No, I hadn't, Phil. And believe me, I don't encourage him either," I went on hastily.

"Perhaps your lack of encouragement intrigues him!" Phil decided. "He is a very personable young man, and I have noticed that he attracts the attention of a number of women."

"You are a very noticing person, aren't you?" I retorted. "However, for your information, Karl Lippe is not my type!"

"I hope I am, Miranda!" he exclaimed. "And I also hope you will give me some encouragement!"

"Idiot!" I laughed. "What are you going on about?"

"It so happens that I have the day off, and I was hoping to persuade you to spend it with me," he wheedled. "I thought of driving up to the Kahlenberg Heights, and perhaps going for a stroll through the Vienna Woods. Does that appeal to you?"

"Oh!" A little bubble of delight rose to my throat and almost choked me. "I should love that! But what about Sula?" The question was out before I could stop myself uttering the words.

"Sula?" he said in surprise. "Sula has a rehearsal today, didn't you know?"

"Why no! What is she rehearsing?" I asked. "Don't tell me she is the mystery star who is going to appear in the Ring at the Opera House!"

"Not quite!" he chuckled. "And she isn't playing the lead in Vienna's latest and most daring night club either, if that was to be your next question!

"But seriously, Miranda, didn't Sula tell you what she is doing here, in Vienna? I thought she was bound to, during one of your long, chatty get-togethers."

"I thought she was here on holiday, to keep her father company during his conference."

"Their being here at the same time was a coincidence, albeit a happy one."

"Then why is she here, and what is she rehearsing?" I was curious to know.

"If you promise to come out with me today, I'll tell you!"

I hesitated, not wanting to seem too eager for his company.

"I'll have to look and see what is on our agenda for today. Will you hold on a minute?"

From my earlier study of the program I knew that there was no item on the list which particularly interested me, and even if there had been, the prospect of going out with Phil for the day, and particularly the prospect of going for a walk in the Wienerwald, was a much greater attraction.

"There is nothing special on," I said after a brief pause, "and I would love a walk in the country. I find the atmosphere in the hotel a trifle oppressive, with so many people about all the time. I am not particularly fond of crowds."

"I know what you mean," he sympathized.

"And all the security men who fail to make themselves inconspicuous don't add to the general gaiety. There are times," he went on wryly, "when the conference rooms seem more like concentration camps, there are so many strong-arm men about!"

"Oh!" I exclaimed, with dawning understanding. "I thought in some instances that the male delegates, and some of the female ones too, seemed to have as much brawn as brain. It never occurred to me there were security personnel among us. But why all the fuss?"

"There were the usual rumors last week that someone was going to defect from East to West and vice versa, but the main reason for security being so tight, especially with Sir Jack's lot, is possible kidnappings. Kidnappings on the grand scale by terrorists at international meetings is not uncommon these days, and the Austrians are particularly sensitive after the OPEC affair."

"These thoughts never crossed my mind when I decided to come to Vienna with our delegation!" I gasped. "Phil! You don't think anything like that is going to happen, do you?"

"Of course not," he reassured me, "but it is as well to be prepared. However," he said firmly, "I don't want to waste the morning chatting over the phone. I have still to arrange about hiring a car for the day, unless, of course, you could persuade your Austrian friend to lend us his Porsche?"

"I could just imagine what he would say if I asked him!" I giggled. "She is the love of his life at the moment!"

"In that case, I shall just have to see what Avis or Hertz can do for me," he rejoined lightly. "We can drink coffee in the lounge until the car arrives, so how about joining me there in, say, quarter of an hour?"

I slowly replaced the receiver on its cradle, and with a dreamy smile on my face I waltzed gaily around the bed. It was going to be a lovely, lovely day, no matter what the weather forecaster had said about the prospect of rain and snow later!

I pulled on my fur-lined boots, tucked a bright gold silk scarf into the neckline of the dull gold tunic jersey suit I was wearing, buttoned on my suede coat with its cosy high fur collar, and pulled the matching red fox hat down over my ears. Even if the snow that had been threatening since I had pulled back the bedroom curtains were to arrive, I would be warm and snug for my drive to the Vienna Woods.

Phil had said to meet him in the coffee lounge in a quarter of an hour, but I was too restless and excited to wait in my room. I decided to go down to the shops in the hotel arcade and look for souvenirs. One shop in particular had interested me, with its lovely display of Augarten porcelain, the enamel work for which Vienna is famous, and I felt sure I would find a suitable present for my mother there.

I was trying to decide which of two dainty candleholders I would purchase when I saw Major Dietrich come into the shop. I turned my back to him, hoping that he would not recognize me, but as I stared down at the goods the assistant had put out on the counter for me to choose from, I could not help being aware that he had come up to stand right behind me.

"Can I help you, sir?" the fair-haired assistant asked him.

"*Danke.* I would like to know the price of the little cow bells you have on display in the window."

The girl opened a drawer behind the counter and brought out a box full of cow bells of different sizes and with different designs on them, and quoted various prices to him.

"The smallest bells interest me." He picked one up. "I could put one on the collar of my prowling tom cat, so that I would know where he strayed. Don't you think that would be a good idea, Miss Ogilvie?"

He turned to me, switching to English as he addressed me, and staring directly at me with his cold blue eyes.

"Cats are not easy creatures to bell, or to keep from straying," I replied with a shrug. "They like their independence. But if you keep a cat, you will know that already!"

I turned my attention back to the girl who was waiting for me to make up my mind about the candleholders.

"I am sorry," I smiled at her. "I simply cannot decide which one I want, but I shall come back later with a friend who will help me make the final choice. Thank you very much for your help. *Guten Tag.*"

I walked towards the door, and as I reached the entrance I heard Dietrich say hurriedly, "I shall take this one, Fräulein. Don't bother to wrap it!"

I was half along the arcade which led back into the hotel when I heard rapid footsteps behind me, and glancing around, I saw Dietrich striding after me, as if he wanted to catch up with me.

The major appeared to be overinterested in me, and I wanted nothing to do with him. There was something about his manner which made me feel uneasy, so I quickened my pace and was delighted, on reentering the hotel foyer, to see Phil Hunter standing there waiting for me.

"Hello there!" he smiled. "What's the rush? You came shooting along the arcade as if you were practicing for a walking race! Didn't you think I'd wait for you?"

"It's that Major Dietrich!" I gave a shiver of distaste as I glanced back over my shoulder. "He seems to haunt me! He followed me into a shop just now, and there he is, following me again!"

"You are bound to keep bumping into the same people every now and again, when you are staying in the same hotel." Phil tucked my arm into his. "And in any case, you can stop worrying about Dietrich for the rest of the day! He will have to stay for the conference. It would never do if he walked out on Sir Jack's speech! It would be bad for diplomatic relations and that sort of thing!"

He led me out of the hotel to where a dark green Fiat was parked and opened the passenger door for me to enter.

75

"Your carriage awaits, madame!" he said with a flourish. "May I wish you a pleasant trip?"

His cheerfulness communicated itself to me, and as we chatted lightheartedly of this and that as we drove along I soon forgot the sinister major.

Ignoring the weather forecast, the sun came out from behind the clouds, thinning them out, and the morning grew bright as we drove along the Heiligenstadterstrasse, on our way to the Kahlenberg Heights.

"I suppose you have been to the Wienerwald before?" Phil asked.

I nodded. "A crowd of us often took the tram to Grinzing of an evening, and we would sit out in the garden cafés, listening to the music and talking and arguing about everything under the sun!" I smiled reminiscently. "Fortunately, we always managed to be in time for the 'last blue'!"

"The last blue?" Phil shot me a puzzled look.

"The last tram," I explained. "It's so called because it has a blue rear light, which they say winks maliciously at those who miss it, as it goes careering downhill out of sight!"

"Didn't Rudi have a car in those days?" he asked innocently, but I ignored his question and put one of my own.

"You said you were going to tell me why Sula is here in Vienna," I reminded him. "I have been dying with curiosity to know what it is she is rehearsing today."

"Sula is a fashion model," he told me. "Are you sure you didn't know?" he glanced at me with a frown. "She has often appeared in *Vogue*."

"It's the clothes I look at when I buy a fashion magazine," I replied. "I'm afraid I don't pay much attention to the models who wear them."

He gave me a quick look to see if I was in earnest.

"It's true, Phil. It is the cut of the clothes, and to find out what are the new colors for the season, and wonder if they will suit me, that interest me. Still, I suppose a man would pay more attention to the model than to the clothes she is showing off!"

"I wonder what Sula would think of that remark!" He seemed amused.

"What fashion house is she modeling for here?" I inquired.

"Aldo Giovane, or some such name. It's a new fashion house, and they are arranging a special opening display in the Mahler tomorrow afternoon. Sula says they want everything to go like clockwork, hence all the rehearsals."

"I'd love to see a spectacular fashion show!" I sighed.

"I am sure Sula could get you a ticket."

"I'd have to see what's on at the conference first. I can't play truant all the time," I said slowly. "But it would be very tempting, if I could get a ticket."

We crossed the Kierlingbach and after a short climb we came to Klosterneuburg Abbey, which contains the beautiful Verdun altarpiece, one of the most magnificent enamel works of the Middle Ages, and then went on over the Weidlingbach valley to the Hohenstrasse, where the road wound upwards between lovely villas to enter the Vienna Woods.

We stopped every now and then to admire the views which opened out to us of the Abbey and the Danube far below, before driving on to the Kahlenberg restaurant, whose terrace overlooks the city of Vienna.

"I have always loved this view," I turned to Phil with a smile. "You can see over the whole city and pick out each landmark. Thank goodness the snow which was forecast for today did not materialize!"

"So you didn't mind coming to see it again?" Phil looked at me. "I did not realize, when I asked you to come here for the day, that you had visited the spot so often before." He sounded disappointed.

"The view from here never seems the same, and today, for some reason, I think it lovelier than ever," I reassured him. "The winter sunshine somehow adds to the charm. It isn't so blatant as in summer, and the paler light gives the scene a gentler, more luminous quality, if you know what I mean."

We ate our lunch overlooking the city, and although we could see the dark clouds of the predicted storm building up in the east, we had come to enjoy fresh air and a walk through the Vienna Woods, and this we intended to do. Phil assured me that his knowledge of weather conditions told him that the tempest would not reach this area until late afternoon.

It was very pleasant strolling through the

trees. The cold air seemed to enhance the sweet smell of damp earth and pine needles, and the sun continued to filter bravely through the branches, casting a lacy pattern over the track we were following.

"I can never quite believe the Wienerwald is real," I said, bending down to pick up a pretty cone, which was still resilient to the touch, and had the golden gleam of this year's harvest, in contrast to the darker, more brittle cones that poked out from the dying grasses.

I put it in my handbag, and Phil smiled.

"What did you do that for?" he asked.

I flushed faintly with embarrassment.

"I like collecting souvenirs of a special day's outing," I mumbled.

"How many cones have you already collected from this wood?" he asked with a teasing smile. "I expect you came along this track quite often with Rudi of a summer's evening?"

"We occasionally came up here from Grinzing," I replied, although I did not enlighten him that "we" was a crowd of fellow students, and not just Rudi and I, "but we didn't do a lot of walking, and it was pleasant to sit on the terrace, listening to the music and singing and enjoying an 'achtel Gespritzt'!"

I sighed. "All that seems such a very long time ago!"

"What is 'achtel Gespritzt'?" queried Phil. "It sounds very exotic!"

"It's a glass made up half of white wine and half of soda water, and it is most refreshing.

What is more, you can make a glass last a very long time!"

Phil bent down to pick up another small cone, which was still attached to the twig on which it had grown.

"Look, Miranda! This cone is even prettier than the cone you found! Let it be a souvenir from me to you!"

He stepped in front of me so that I had to stop walking, and with a smile he pulled the stalk of the larch twig through the buttonhole of my coat, tugging it to make sure that it was firmly in position.

"There!" he seemed satisfied. "It looks well there, even if it is a darker shade of brown-gold than your coat. In fact," he looked at it again, "it is almost the same whiskey color of the hair you have tucked out of sight under that very becoming hat you are wearing."

He continued to look at me with a speculative gleam in his eyes.

"You know, Miranda Ogilvie," he pronounced slowly, "you yourself would make a very pretty model, and it would not be the clothes you wore, but that innocent, wide-eyed look of yours that would attract attention!"

His eyes narrowed. "Tell me, Miranda, are you as innocent as you appear to be, with that heavenly blue gaze of yours?"

I flushed angrily. "I don't know what you are driving at!"

"You have traveled a lot, I gather. You are intelligent. You are very attractive to look at. How come you are not married, or at least engaged?" His glance strayed to my gloved left hand as if to indicate that he had previously noticed it to be ringless.

"I have no desire to get married, or to form any attachment until I have made something of my career. The one would interfere with the other, and that would not be fair to either."

"Surely you could be a successful writer and wife at the same time?"

"I am only a part-time writer," I pointed out. "My actual job is as librarian in a college library, and I hope to be in on the ground floor of a big reorganization program next year."

"Yes, I see how that could be important to you," he spoke slowly. "As a librarian, by your choice of books you could sway the opinions of the people who come to you for advice on what to read, and what authors to study?"

I gave him a thoughtful look.

"Oddly enough, that idea had not crossed my mind. In any case, there are so many other ways that impressionable minds can be brainwashed these days. Newspapers. Radio. Television. Even advertising. No one has a completely unbiased opinion in any of the media, and I suppose the same thing goes for you and me. We all have our own pet theories as to how other people should act, or what they should think. Yes," I sighed, "I daresay I am as bigoted as anyone when it comes to politics!"

"Oh?" queried Phil, and a gleam of interest came into his eyes as he cast me a speculative look.

"Yes," I nodded my head. "I think that party politics and party politicians should all be exiled to a deserted island where they can try and force their one-sided opinions on each other, and not on the man-in-the-street, who just wants to get on with living an uncomplicated life! Power politics, madmen who think they are gods, megalomaniacs, have killed too many innocents in the past, and are still killing them, openly or in secret. I have no time at all for politicians with selfish ends.

"There, you see!" I gave him a wry smile. "I myself am bigoted against politics and politicians!"

Phil gave me an amused glance.

"I think you could do with a glass of your 'achtel Gespritzt' to cool you down, after that little speech," he stated, with a cheerful lilt in his voice. "Politics certainly do seem to get you het up!

"All the same," he chuckled, "you had better not let your *bête noire* Major Dietrich hear you air such views! He would think you an even more subversive influence on young Karl Lippe than he already considers you to be, with your elegant western clothes, your seductive Paris perfume, and that bewitching smile of yours!"

"Now you are making fun of me!" I pouted. "But I did mean what I have just said. Let's banish all politicians to a remote island, and that goes doubly for my sinister-looking Major Dietrich!

"But Phil," I touched his arm and smiled up

82

at him, "we came here to wander through my favorite woods, not to talk of my unfavorite subject!"

Chapter Seven

We agreed to abandon serious discussions for the remainder of the afternoon, and strolled on through the trees in amiable silence. At one point, Phil took hold of my hand to help me climb a grassy bank so that we could have a better view of the sweep of the Danube and the southward stretch of the Wienerwald as it merged into the distant hills, and he continued to hold my hand in his warm clasp when we returned to the path to make our way back to the spot where we had parked the car.

A fine mist was beginning to swirl lightly around the boles of the trees and across the path, and the sun, gleaming less brightly than heretofore, was more silver than gold and gave an air of unreality to the scene.

"Any moment now," I smiled up at Phil, "a horse-drawn fiacre will appear, and we shall see Arthur Schnitzler and his ladylove in it!"

"Or more romantically," Phil gripped my fingers more tightly, "we might see Emperor Franz Josef and his lovely Empress Elisabeth!"

"Or perhaps it will be the tragic lovers, the Archduke Rudolf and pretty little Maria Vetsera, on one of their happier rides, before the tragedy of Mayerling!" I continued the fantasy.

"Somehow," I went on, with a sigh, "it is difficult to think of Vienna and tragedy, although there have been so many associated with it, even," I went from the sublime to the ridiculous, "poor Ivy's death, and the young chambermaid's murder!"

"Don't get morbid, my love!" Phil remonstrated lightly as we reached the car. "And you must never think of Vienna as a city of tragedy! The Viennese would not like it! To them Vienna is a city of romance; a city of music; a city of dreams; a city of the future, even! They want to put tragedies and the Third Man image behind them."

I took a long, lingering look at the scene stretched out before me. The haze was thickening in the valleys and the louring clouds were fast closing in on us, yet in spite of the threatening weather I was reluctant to return to Vienna and the Mahler with its international guests and its international chatter.

I had enjoyed the stroll through the woods, the conversation, and above all the inexplicable pleasure I invariably experienced in Phil Hunter's company. Although we had known each other for only a few days, we were very much at ease in each other's company, and even silences between us were not awkward ones.

"Let's stop for coffee on the way home!" I suggested to him as we neared Grinzing. "An Einspänner and a Mohnstrudel would make a pleasant Viennese ending to our pleasant afternoon!"

Phil shot a quick glance at his watch.

"I am sorry, Miranda," he said apologetically.

"That would have been a very pleasant way to round off the afternoon, but I must be back at the Mahler before four o'clock. It will take us all our time to get there as it is. I had not realized how long we lingered in the woods."

"It has been a most enjoyable day, Phil, afternoon coffee or no afternoon coffee!" I smiled at him. "It was nice of you to invite me with you."

"We both needed to get away from business for a few hours. The afternoon has been like a tonic for me!"

For a time we sat in silence as we drove down the steep, twisting road, past the vineyards where the Emperor Probus planted the first vine many centuries ago, and down, down, to the outskirts of Vienna and the city itself, where we were delayed by the congestion of the afternoon rush-hour traffic and the slipperiness of the roads caused by the mixture of rain, sleet and snow which was now falling quite heavily.

As we advanced yard by slow yard, Phil kept glancing at his watch, as if his worried looks could make time stand still for him.

"I had no idea the streets would be so busy at this hour!" he muttered, beating an impatient tattoo on the steering wheel with his fingers. "If I had known there was going to be such a hold-up, I wouldn't have wasted so much time dilly-dallying in the woods!"

I was conscious of a warm flush of annoyance creeping over my body, and I had to make an effort to bite back the angry retort which rose to my lips.

I hadn't suggested the walk. I hadn't forced

Phil to loiter in the woods, admiring the various views they opened on to, and I had not sulked, as I guessed Sula would have done, when he had turned down my suggestion that we should stop somewhere along the road for coffee and cake, so he was not justified in putting the blame on me for being caught in the present traffic jam.

I glared angrily ahead of me as we moved another few yards, only to be held up again, this time by traffic lights. From the moment I had arrived in Vienna, each pleasant outing I had, had finished in a manner which had taken some of the gilt from the occasion, and now I felt near to tears because this special day was following the same pattern.

With the change for the worse in the weather, there had been a dramatic change from daylight to near blackness in a matter of minutes. Motorists had been forced to switch on their car headlights, and the beamed rays served to make the dreary darkness more oppressive. It was almost as if the weather was in tune with my thoughts, plumeting from lightheartedness to depression in a few minutes, and without realizing I was expressing my feelings aloud, I sighed deeply.

Phil shot me a swift look.

"I am sorry, Miranda," he spoke in a shamed voice, and taking one hand off the wheel he closed it over mine.

"I am a bad-tempered so-and-so at times, and as impatient as they come, as my friends and family could tell you!"

Our eyes met in the driving mirror, and the way he smiled at me did peculiar things to my heartbeat, setting it racing wildly, and making me very conscious of the pressure of his hand on mine and of how much I was growing to like this man who was seated beside me.

"I didn't mean what I said about wasting time dilly-dallying in the woods," he went on, giving my fingers another squeeze before withdrawing his hand to put the car into a higher gear as we managed to slip into a less-congested side street away from the main buildup of traffic. "It was very pleasant. Very pleasant indeed!"

The wind was increasing in strength, and the sleet was turning to a wet snow which transformed the streets into slushy quagmires that had to be negotiated with care.

Phil stopped the car under the stone canopy which stretched across the private road that ran the length of the hotel front.

"You can get out here," he said. "I shall take the car around to the hotel garage, and then I shall have to dash to keep my appointment."

He leaned across me to open the door for me.

"Goodbye for now," he smiled at me as I got out of the car. "I hope to see you this evening in the cocktail bar at the usual time!"

I entered the hotel as the afternoon sessions of the two conferences were finishing. Delegates came drifting from the halls in groups of twos and threes, and while some hurried to the elevators to return to their rooms, others lingered in the reception hall to argue over the topics of the day, or to wait for friends, but the majority made their way to one or the other of the hotel cafés.

I caught sight of Mabel and Senga talking animatedly to their usual attendants, but fortunately they had not noticed me.

They would have wanted to know where I had been and what I had been doing with myself, since I had attended neither of the day's meetings, and when they learned that I had spent the day with Phil Hunter, there would have been raised eyebrows and knowing looks, and I was not in the mood for this. I wanted to keep my pleasant memories of the day to myself, and without consciously doing so, my hand moved up to the top button of my coat, just below the fur collar, to touch the sprig of larch, with its tiny cone, which Phil had fastened there. This was definitely a sprig which would be put in my box of happy holiday souvenirs when I got back home.

Although I had a pang of conscience at deliberately avoiding the two women who had been so friendly and helpful towards me these past few days, I lurked behind one of the enormous rubber plants in the hall to find out which of the cafés they were making for, and when I saw them walk towards the one on the mezzanine floor, I hurried into the arcade, to go to the café which looked out on the street.

As I entered the café, I saw Sula Neilson, who was seated at a table beside the window, talking to an effeminate-looking man wearing a purple velvet jacket over a canary yellow silk shirt, which had a flouncing canary-yellow tie to match. His carefully styled wavy hair was almost the same shade as his shirt, and on his little finger he wore a broad gold ring set with a large purple amethyst which sparkled in the light as he waved his hand about to stress some point in his conversation.

The only vacant table in the room was at the window beside them, and I hurried towards it. I had had an early lunch in the restaurant on the Heights which overlooked Vienna, and this factor, coupled with the long walk Phil and I had taken through the woods in the cold, fresh air, was responsible for the urgent desire I had for something substantial to eat.

Sula happened to glance towards the entrance, and she saw me walk across the room. Without hesitation she signaled to me to come over to join her and her friend at the table where they were seated.

"Do sit with us, Miranda," she invited as I reached the table. "Unless, of course," she gave me a mischievous look, "you were hurrying to keep the table next to us free for your friend Karl and his two henchmen!"

I turned around cautiously, and saw that the two Lippes and Major Dietrich were only a couple of yards behind me and obviously making for the table that I had originally been heading for.

Their arrival left me in no doubts about accepting Sula's invitation, for I certainly did not wish to share a table with them!

"You are sure I am not butting into a private conversation?" I looked down at Sula.

"On the contrary," she replied. "I am delighted to see you! We are tired of talking shop—at least I am."

I sat down beside Sula with my back to the table at which Karl Lippe and his friends were now sitting.

"It's a pity the weather broke when it did," Sula sighed as she stared out of the window at the sleet-swept road. "I had been hoping to do some window-shopping in the Kärntnerstrasse. There are some fabulous places there—fashion shops, jeweler's shops, and a place which specializes in crystal!"

"Darling," simpered the man opposite her, "you haven't introduced me to your friend!"

"I'm sorry! I forgot that you two hadn't already met. Miranda, this is Aldo Giovane, who creates the most gorgeous clothes for women, and who has invited me here to show them off. Aldo, this is Miranda Ogilvie, who is one of the horde of writers one keeps bumping into in the hotel this week!"

We acknowledged the introductions, and Aldo continued to study me with his strange, yellowish eyes, but it was more my clothes than my actual appearance that he was interested in.

"You aren't by any chance a fashion writer?" he queried hopefully after a time. "This new venture of mine needs as much publicity as possible, to get it off the ground." He spoke frankly. "Establishing a new haute couture establishment these days is not easy, even in a fashion-conscious city like Vienna."

"I am sorry I can't help you," I shook my head. "I am a novelist, not a journalist."

"That is a pity." He fidgeted about in his

chair. "But you will come to our show tomorrow, and bring your friends?"

"I should like to," I nodded, and turned to Sula.

"I had no idea you were in Vienna on business, Sula. I was most surprised when Phil explained why you couldn't come with us today."

"Surely you didn't think I was here on holiday at this time of year!" She looked out of the window and gave a shiver. "I prefer lots of sunshine and warmth when I am on vacation."

"I thought you were here as your father's guest—to keep an eye on him and guard him from the seductive wiles of his female colleagues!"

Sula giggled. "I leave that sort of thing to Phil and his friends! And talking of Phil, how did the trip to the Vienna Woods go?"

"I enjoyed it very much, and we were lucky, too, because we were able to go for quite a long walk, and enjoy the views over Vienna, before the weather broke."

I ordered a coffee from the waitress who had come to take my order, and I selected an enormous slice of cream-filled chocolate torte from the cake trolley.

Aldo's eyes widened as the waitress placed it carefully on my plate with the cake tongs, and I thought they would pop completely out of their sockets when Sula, with a quick flicker of her long lashes in my direction, said to the girl:

"I'll have the same, please!"

"My dear!" he moaned with shock. "You can't! Think of your precious waistline!"

Sula made a face at him.

"I don't need to, Aldo. I'm one of the lucky ones!" she said cheerfully. "I can eat and eat and never put on an ounce!"

She forked a pile of the luscious cake into her mouth, and Aldo groaned again.

"I can't bear to watch!" He turned away, and his hands fluttered in a gesture of despair. "I can almost see the inches grow as you swallow the stuff! It's obscene!"

He stood up and signaled the waitress. In spite of my protest, he insisted that what I had taken should be added to his bill. He carefully counted out the correct amount of money, handed it to the girl, and with another disgusted look at the rich cake on Sula's plate, he took his leave of us.

"Poor Aldo!" Sula smiled. "He takes this fashion business very seriously, and actually he is a genius when it comes to new designs and the best fabrics to show them off, as you will see if you come to the show tomorrow, but he has only the one subject of conversation, and I do get tired of talking nonstop shop! Your arrival was a godsend!"

"I hope I didn't chase him away," I frowned.

"Good heavens, no! He was telling the truth when he said he couldn't bear to see me enjoying this confection!" She laughed as she forked another piece of cake into her mouth.

"Talking of talking shop," she went on, "I hope Phil didn't annoy you with all the questions I bet he asked you?" Her voice fell to a whisper. "Actually, he is very intrigued by the attraction you have for the young man sitting behind us, and being security-minded, he would no doubt try to find out if you had known each other before coming to Vienna."

I shot her a puzzled look.

"Why should it bother Phil if I knew Karl before? Why is he so interested in the people I knew on my former visit here?"

"It's his job," replied Sula. "Why else do you think he was taking such an interest in you?" she asked with amusement.

I furrowed my brows.

"I'm afraid I don't understand."

"Why, I thought you would have guessed that Phil is one of the Special Branch men sent to keep an eye on Daddy and his colleagues—but especially on Daddy, because of the specialized work he is doing. It would never do if he were kidnapped, or hijacked or something of the sort! That is why the place is simply bristling with security men, as you may have noticed!"

"Phil mentioned that there were lots of security men about," I said slowly, "but he did not mention that he was one of them. He only said that he was in Vienna on business. He could have told me what his business was!" I ended indignantly.

"It's a wonder you didn't guess, after all the questions I am sure he asked you this afternoon. He would file away all your answers in that computer of his he calls a brain," she shrugged. "A girl can't have a hidden romantic and mysterious past when she goes out with Phil. He automatically checks her background!"

I stirred my coffee thoughtfully. I was not sure how to take Sula's remarks. How much of what she had told me was true, and how much subtle undermining of my confidence, because she was annoyed that Phil had taken me out for the day?

Had Phil's invitation to the Kahlenberg Heights been a casual one, such as a young man makes to a young woman whose company he enjoys, or was Sula correct in hinting that he had asked me out in order to probe with casual guile into my background?

As I scooped a piece of rich chocolate sponge and icing into my mouth, I thought back to the conversations Phil and I had had at various times during the day, and I realized how much I had told him about myself and my family and my ambitions, while learning very little about him in return.

But he hadn't actually asked me for the information, I tried to reassure myself. I had proffered it. Or had I? I bit my lip in thought. Had I been skilfully led into revealing attitudes of mind and other things about myself which I would not normally have discussed with a casual acquaintance, by someone who, by reason of his work, was an expert in the field of subtle interrogation?

The sweetness of the cream cake turned sour in my mouth at the thought that it had been business, rather than pleasure, which had prompted Phil Hunter to take me to the romantic Vienna Woods that day.

I should have known that a man who was on

terms of friendly intimacy with a girl as lovely and sophisticated and amusing as Sula Neilson, would not be tempted to date another woman unless he had a very special reason for doing so.

In my case, the special reason had been a business one, and not, as I had thought, a social one.

To Phil Hunter, I was merely a contact of Sir Jack Neilson, who appeared to have something to do with a handsome man from behind the Iron Curtain, and who consequently had to be carefully vetted, and not a young woman whom he found as interesting, pleasant, and disturbingly attractive as she found him.

Chapter Eight

Although my companion had indicated, when she invited me to sit with her, that she was glad of the opportunity not to talk shop, once she had subtly dropped the pebble of doubt in my mind, to start the ripples of suspicion as to the true nature of Phil Hunter's interest in me, she reverted to chatting about the world of fashion in which she moved.

However, I listened only half-heartedly to Sula's tales about her job, and the people she met in the course of it, and what went on behind the scenes of the elegant showings of each new season's model gowns, although normally I would have absorbed the technical information and the amusing incidents she related like a sponge, to squeeze them out again for my own use at some time in the future as background material for a novel.

My attention wandered to consider my past, present and possible future relationship with the man whose company I had enjoyed so much that day.

If Phil had sought me out merely to test me as a suspect for heaven only knew what plot against his protégé, I did not think I would ever again be able to act naturally in his company. Every casual word I uttered might be assessed for meanings I didn't intend it to have, and I would be so on guard lest I say the wrong thing that conversation would be awkward and stilted.

Moreover, I had foolishly let my guard slip on occasion, when he had smiled at me with what I thought had been growing affection, and when he had taken my hand in his and squeezed my fingers, I had responded to the gesture, so that he must have guessed that I enjoyed his company more than a little—unless, of course, he thought my natural reactions were also worthy of suspicion!

I jabbed my pastry fork viciously into the last morsel of cake, and the prong made such a hideous, screeching noise on the plate that both Sula and I gave a start, and Karl Lippe, who was seated at the next table, turned around, his broad shoulders brushing against the fur collar of my coat as he did so, automatically attracting my attention so that I glanced at him.

As I did so, he grasped the opportunity to speak to me.

"Good afternoon, Miss Ogilvie," he spoke in

English. "It is very nice to see you again. Are your meetings going well?"

His eyes held my gaze as he spoke, and I found it difficult to look away from him.

"Why, yes," I stuttered. "Yes, they are going very well. Although I must confess," I added, "that today I played hooky and went to see the view over Vienna from the Kahlenberg Heights."

Lippe turned his chair around so that he could talk to me with greater ease.

"Hooky?" he frowned. "I do not know the word. What does it mean?" he inquired.

"It's American slang, I believe," I told him, "and it means to play truant."

"I must remember that. Hooky." He repeated the word as if to impress it on his memory file.

"I do not suppose that the view would be very good on a day like this," Major Dietrich interrupted. "You should come back to Vienna in summer, Miss Ogilvie. Then you would see Vienna and its surrounding countryside at their best. But please," he glanced at Karl Lippe with an admonitory frown, "we are interrupting a private conversation. That is not very polite of us!"

Deliberately he turned away, leaving Karl little option but to do the same.

Sula giggled, and said to me in a low whisper, "Dietrich is more like a sergeant major than a major, the way he makes your boyfriend jump to attention!"

"He is not my boyfriend!" I hissed with annoyance. "And for goodness' sake, let us get away from here, before he tries to start up another conversation!"

Sula was in a teasing mood. She smiled a brilliant smile at the three men at the next table as she stood up and wished them a pleasant afternoon, adding that we would no doubt see them later that evening in the cocktail bar.

Inwardly I was vexed by her mischievous behavior, but I had to force a smile at them as I followed Sula, for I did not wish to appear churlish.

"You know, Miranda," chuckled Sula as we left the café, "Phil would have been interested in that little episode. In fact, with his suspicious nature, he might even have thought that you arranged to meet Karl in the café. I know he is disturbed by that young man's interest in you!"

"For goodness' sake, Sula!" I said indignantly. "Phil Hunter has no cause to be suspicious of my actions! In any case," I added, "I can speak to whomever I like and whenever I like! I don't give a damn what he thinks!"

"Actually," Sula shook her head, "I doubt if you will get very many opportunities to chat up your handsome blond Lothario. Old Dietrich doesn't seem to approve of the incipient friendship either!"

We walked together through the arcade, and as we passed the shop in which I had spent some time that morning looking at the porcelain wares, I remembered that I had promised the assistant that I would return later to tell her which piece I had decided to choose.

I asked Sula if she would like to come into the shop with me to help me make up my mind about what I was going to buy. She was very pleased to do so, and we spent some time browsing over the other goods on display in the shop before going into the boutique next door to it, where Sula was anxious to look at belts and handbags.

Sula was very pernickety about what she wanted, and examined every belt which was shown to her with great care, taking color, breadth, material, texture, and finish into consideration. Finally she selected a narrow snakeskin one with a snakehead clasp, and as she was paying for it she told the assistant that she would return to the boutique the next day to look at the handbags, and particularly the snakeskin ones.

As we left the shop, she glanced at her watch, and then said to me, "Miranda, I'm sorry, but I shall have to leave you now. I promised Father I would meet him after the committee meeting in the president's room, and that should be over by now. We usually go for coffee about now— Aldo doesn't approve of this continual coffee drinking of mine," she interjected with a smile, "but it's one way of passing the time, and I expect Phil will be there too," she mentioned casually. "I shall tell him that you are bearing up very well after the ordeal of his interrogation this afternoon!"

She hurried off and I stood staring after her, biting my lip in vexation at her final remark.

Sula did not need to stress that Phil Hunter's

interest in me was purely a professional one. She had already made it quite clear that this was the case, as well as stressing the fact that Phil and she were on very friendly terms.

I watched her make for the elevator hall as I lingered irresolutely in the shopping arcade. I had originally intended, after we parted company, to go to my room and do some work on my current novel, but now I felt too restless to sit down at the desk, and even if I did, I doubted if I would be able to concentrate on my writing.

A walk in the fresh air was what I needed. A good, brisk breeze on my face would blow away the cobwebs and help me think clearly again. However, the storm of sleet and snow was still raging outside, and I was forced to discard this idea. There was no point in trudging through slush, ruining my new boots, and getting my coat soaked through, just in order to clear my head of my confused feelings for a man I hardly knew; a man who, however much he attracted me, I knew to have no interest in me as a woman; a man who, for some reason or other, according to Sula, seemed to think I was up to no good.

I gazed disconsolately into the window of the boutique where Sula had bought her belt, wondering what to do with myself.

There was no official function on the agenda of the International Novelists Conference for this particular evening, and a long, lonely and boring evening stretched ahead for me.

Phil Hunter had suggested, when he had left me at the hotel entrance after our drive, that I should meet him and his friends, as I had done on the previous evening, in the cocktail bar at the usual time, which I took to be eight o'clock, but now I was not sure if I should take him up on what was possibly a polite suggestion rather than a pressing invitation.

To kill a few more minutes, I went into the book shop beside the café and glanced through the selection of titles on display, finally deciding to buy a beautifully illustrated guidebook to Vienna, which I would be able to study at my leisure later in the evening.

Clutching my parcel, I made my way to the elevators, where a group of my fellow guests stood waiting to be whisked up to their rooms.

I was about to step into the elevator when I remembered I had not retrieved my room key from the reception desk. I went to get it, but the assistants were busy and I had to wait for a minute or so before I was able to attract attention.

A malicious whim of fate must surely have been responsible for the delay, for when I returned to the elevator hall, the Lippes were standing there with some of their fellow delegates.

Karl smiled at me, but his father moved between us, and I gathered from the way he turned his back on me and ignored me that he did not approve of his son's interest in me any more than did Major Dietrich, who on this occasion was surprisingly absent from Karl's side!

Marguerite Dupont, the international secretary of the Novelists Association, came rushing towards the elevator as the doors were about to close, and squashed in beside me.

She smiled at me, recognizing me as a member of the British delegation, and said:

"I have just been along to the hospital to inquire after your countrywoman, Dorinda Grey."

I gave a guilty start.

In my selfishness, first in my delight at being asked to spend the greater part of the day with Phil Hunter, then in my bitterness when I had discovered that his interest in me was quite impersonal, I had forgotten about Dorinda and her accident!

"How is she?" I asked. "I haven't seen any of my writing friends today, to ask about her condition."

Marguerite shrugged and her deep amber eyes clouded over.

"*Hélas*, she is not so well! However, they were expecting this slight relapse in her condition, and they assure me there is nothing to worry about.

"She still has no recollection of the accident, or indeed, of any of the events of the past few days, and she was quite bewildered to find herself in a hospital in Vienna, the first time she came around!"

The Frenchwoman shook her head. "Can you imagine it! She did not remember leaving her home and doesn't understand why she should now be in Vienna!"

"How awful for her!" I gasped. "I can imagine what a shock it would be, on top of everything else, to open your eyes in a foreign land, having no idea how you got there!"

"This loss of memory is one of the reasons the doctors are debarring all visitors meantime," said Marguerite. "They don't want her to be worried with questions, or to be forced to remember things."

"How long will the amnesia last?" I inquired.

"The doctors won't commit themselves, but they hint at least a week, and as a matter of fact they also said that it is quite possible that the memory blank for the day immediately preceding the accident could continue for weeks, or even forever!"

The elevator stopped at the tenth floor, and with a smile, and expressing the hope that we might see each other later for a chat, Marguerite Dupont got out of the elevator, followed by several other people, including the elder Lippe. Karl Lippe, however, made no move to follow his father, a fact of which the older man was not aware until the door of the elevator was almost closed again.

I had a momentary glimpse of the dropping of his jaw in utter astonishment as he gaped through the fast-closing aperture, and then I heard his son give a chuckle of triumph as he turned to address me.

"Now that for once I have managed to be alone with you, Miss Ogilvie, may I ask you if you will return with me to the café, where we can sit and talk together?"

The elevator stopped at the eleventh floor, the door slid open, but before I could step out, he moved boldly in front of me, barring my way, and pressed the button for the car to descend once again to the ground floor!

For a brief second I was annoyed at his behavior, but annoyance soon gave way to amusement. Karl had more spirit than I had credited him with! What was more, it was nice to think that here was a pleasant man who wanted to spend some time in my company because he found me attractive, not because it was his duty to find out more about me, as in Phil Hunter's case. He had also gone to the length of displeasing his father and his guardian angel, Major Dietrich, who I could imagine would be extremely annoyed when he learned of his behavior.

"You aren't giving me much choice, are you, Herr Lippe?" I smiled at him. "I feel as if I am being kidnapped!"

"Please! I don't want you to be upset!" he spoke seriously. "But I had to act quickly, you understand?"

I nodded with a smile and remarked, "Yes! I have noticed that your duennas, or whatever the male counterpart of a duenna is called, don't like to let you out of their sight."

From the puzzled look on his face, I could see that he did not fully understand what I meant, so before he asked me to explain, I added quickly, "It is kind of you to invite me for a coffee, Mr. Lippe. Talking to you will be more entertaining than sitting alone in my room, reading this guidebook on Vienna," I tapped the parcel I was holding, "which is what I was planning to do."

"Ah! So you do not have an appointment with your man, Herr—Herr Hunter?"

I smiled cheerfully.

"Like you yourself, Mr. Lippe, Mr. Hunter is only a casual acquaintance; someone I met for the first time the other evening on my arrival at the Mahler," I enlightened him. "He is a friend of Sula Neilson, the pretty girl I was drinking coffee with a short time ago."

"So!" He let out a long breath of satisfaction. "That is good, then!"

As the elevator passed the second floor stage, he quickly put his finger on the button for the mezzanine floor.

"I have changed my mind. We shall go to the café here," he announced as the elevator stopped seconds later and the door slid open. "It is more private, less open to the view from the road and the arcade like the other one down on the ground floor."

He took my arm firmly and hustled me along the broad corridor to a wood-paneled room right at the far end, from which I could hear the rattle of china and the buzz of conversation.

We entered the room at the same time that Phil Hunter was leaving it. At first he did not notice me, for he was deep in conversation with a man who was a stranger to me.

I did not know whether to be sorry or pleased not to be seen by him. In one way I was glad, because I knew that for some reason he did not approve of the way Karl dogged my footsteps, and he would be disappointed because I had ignored his advice about Lippe. On the other hand, having learned that he himself was only interested in me from his professional point of view, it would have pleased me to let him see that not only was I not dependent on him for male company, but I was also not going to let myself be influenced by him as to the company I kept.

It was Karl who actually drew Phil's attention to us, and he did it quite deliberately, almost as if he was crowing over Phil because I was his companion.

"Good day, Mr. Hunter!" he boomed in his deep voice. "I did not see you at the meeting today. Were the speakers not of interest to you?"

Phil looked up, and catching sight of me standing beside Karl, who was still holding my arm, his eyes narrowed.

"Good afternoon, Mr. Lippe," he acknowledged the greeting. "I had other interesting business to attend to today!" He flicked me a cool look before turning his attention back to Karl and saying with a hint of malice in his tone, "How come you have managed to slip your guard dogs?"

Karl's fair skin flushed to an unbecoming shade of pink.

"I do not understand you!" he shook his head. "You joke?"

"I joke!" agreed Phil, but there was a complete lack of humor in the glance he shot me as he added, "I hope you and Miss Ogilvie will enjoy a pleasant discussion on politics. She has very definite ideas on the subject!"

Karl frowned as he urged me ahead of him towards a vacant table.

"What did Mr. Hunter mean by that? Are you deeply interested in politics?" he asked in a troubled voice.

"Mr. Hunter has a peculiar sense of humor," I assured him. "He knows that politics bore me, so remember, Karl," I gave him my most charming smile, "whatever else we talk about this afternoon, politics is barred!"

"That is good!" he nodded, jutting out his lower lip in agreement. "We shall talk of you and me, but not of our politics, *hein*?"

He signaled a waitress and ordered coffees, and I could not resist a piece of Apfelstrudel from the cake trolley, although Karl himself decided against taking a cake.

We talked about my books to begin with, but I sensed that he was disappointed because they were fiction books, and light fiction at that, so I switched the conversation to our homelands. He asked a great many questions about Scotland, which he had always wanted to visit, and asked me to describe the scenery, which I told him in parts was very like that of the Tyrol. He was also interested in its industry and its literature, and proudly quoted a verse of Burns to me, although he didn't quite get his tongue around some of the words.

In my turn, I asked him about his home country.

"I am afraid I know very little about East Germany, apart from its geographical location," I confessed. "However, I have read a great many articles about your mother, and have often seen photographs of her in our papers and news magazines. She is regarded by us as a fine example of how a woman can make a name for herself in the government of a country, and still remain feminine and charming!" I smiled at him. "You must be very proud of her!"

"Yes, I am!" he nodded. "My mother and her father before her have done a great deal for my country, and are held in very high esteem!"

"Your father is an important man too!" I pointed out. "He is reputed to be extremely brilliant in his field."

Karl's mouth tightened.

"Yes, my father is a clever man. A very clever man!"

I glanced at him sharply. Did I detect a faint sneer in his voice? Was there some difficulty in their relationship? A jealousy about the importance of their respective works? Or was the feeling something to do with Karl's obvious adoration of his mother, an absurd male jealousy between father and son, which no doubt Sigmund Freud would have an explanation for?

Karl must have realized that he had betrayed feelings which he normally kept under control, for he added hurriedly, "Yes, my father is an important man, too. He has done much for our country in the field of physics . . ."

His voice trailed off as he looked across the table at me, studying my face with attention, as if it pleased him more to gaze at me than to discuss his male parent.

"You have very lovely eyes, Miss Ogilvie!" he

announced suddenly. "They are the same color as the blue of the wild flowers that carpet our woods in early summer. The same color as my mother's eyes..."

He continued to stare at me unblinkingly, then a slow frown furrowed his brow.

"I wonder if that is why Major Dietrich keeps looking at you?" He posed the question more to himself than to me. "Yes!" he nodded agreement with his own conclusion. "That could be the reason!

"You see, Miss Ogilvie," he went on to explain, "Dietrich wanted to marry my mother when she was a young girl—a few months before she met my father!" His lips grew tight again.

"He was an upstart. A soldier who had risen rapidly from the ranks because of the postwar conditions. A peasant. A man from nowhere, with no background, no relatives, nothing! A man without finesse—"

"He still hasn't acquired any!" I interrupted, but Karl ignored my exclamation.

"Even in those days, my mother, young as she was, was clever, and of growing importance. She liked a man to have brains and ability, she often told me. She liked a man who had a background so that you could know what to expect of him. She fell in love with my father as much for these things as for his charm, and Dietrich was spurned, swept out of her life."

"I am surprised that he is still friendly with your family."

"Friendly?" he sneered. "The friendliness is on the surface only! Dietrich would do anything to discredit my father, or me, or my mother. He has never forgiven her the insult of passing him over for my father. That is why he is always watching us. He hopes to find some fault in us; he would like to see one or the other of us disgrace ourselves, for in so doing we would bring disgrace on my mother—but he will never succeed. Never!" He banged his fist on the table to emphasize his point, and people at the nearby tables turned to see what was going on.

I felt uncomfortable. There was a definite mother complex here. I pitied the poor girl that Karl would one day decide to marry, for he would compare her at all times and in every way with the woman who had borne him, and I had no doubts that he would find her lacking.

The reason he was attracted to me, he had let slip without realizing he had done so, when he mentioned that the major he so disliked watched me with interest because I reminded him of Karl's mother, the woman who had turned him down.

Carefully I steered the conversation away from personalities and families to a safer discussion of the famous Spanish Riding School and its origins, and of the performance of the Lipizzan stallions which we had enjoyed the previous evening.

However, after a time I found conversation with Karl, who spoke English in a rather old-fashioned, overcorrect style, somewhat heavy going, and for once I was pleased to see the arrival of Major Dietrich, who appeared in the doorway of the café and stood there, glowering, until he eventually caught sight of Karl and me. When he had done so he attracted Karl's attention with a wave of his hand, and then tapped on his wrist watch as if to indicate to my companion that it was time he reported back for duty.

Chapter Nine

Instead of waiting in the hall for Karl to come to him, Major Dietrich came striding towards our table. He might have suspected there could be another show of mutiny on my companion's part, and was going to make sure that this did not happen.

"Mr. Hunter told me I would find you here!" he barked. "It is as well I saw him."

He looked down at Karl with an angry glance before turning to me and saying with a stiff bow, "Good evening, Miss Ogilvie. I am sorry to interrupt your conversation, but Herr Lippe has a meeting to attend. Come, Karl!" He tapped the young man on the shoulder.

Karl glowered, but obeyed. Rising to his feet, he looked down at me.

"You must excuse me, Miss Ogilvie, but I have to go to this unexpected meeting." His tone softened as he added, "I have enjoyed our chat. I found all that you told me about your country most interesting and I would have liked to learn more about it, but I mustn't keep Major Dietrich waiting!"

His eyes, still staring into mine, seemed to be willing me to remember what he had told me earlier about his relationship with the older man, and how he was forced by circumstances to be on his best behavior with him. However, to show he was not completely dominated by Dietrich he went on, "Perhaps we shall meet for another coffee sometime, *ja?*"

I smiled at him and stood up to walk with him to the hallway. "That would be very pleasant," I assured him, but my reply was made more to irritate the pompous soldier who delighted in keeping Karl under his thumb than because I was eager to continue my acquaintanceship with the young man. Karl was pleasant enough, but not my type. I found him somewhat stiff in manner and utterly devoid of humor. The only time he came to life was when he was talking of his mother. She must be quite a person, I thought, not only to have reached the heights she had reached in her country's government, but also because of the spell she seemed to have cast over the three men I had met here in Vienna, who had all played, and were still playing, such an important part in her life.

I cast a swift sideways glance at Major Dietrich and turned very quickly away again, for he was regarding me with his usual unblinking stare, as if there was something about me which he found fascinating.

I wondered if Karl was right in ascribing the major's interest in me to the fact that I bore a vague resemblance to his mother. It did not seem very probable. To me he appeared a rather stolid, portly little man with no charm of manner, whose main interest in life was a zealous desire to be on duty for his country twenty-four hours of the day! The very idea that such a man could carry a torch for a woman for over thirty years, to the extent that he was immediately intrigued by another woman who reminded him of her, seemed quite absurd.

We entered an elevator together, but this time, when the car stopped at the tenth floor, Karl did not repeat his former dodge but stepped out briskly ahead of Dietrich, turning to wish me a brief *"Wiedersehn"* as he left.

It had been quite a day, I decided, as I unlocked my room door, unbuttoned my coat and placed it on a hanger in the hanging wardrobe which stretched the length of the corridor that led into the room.

I placed the small spray of larch, with its gold-brown cone, which Phil had given me, on the dressing table, and sat down on the dressing stool, looking at the cone with a rueful expression.

When Phil had given it to me, I had felt a thrill of happiness. There had been an intimacy about the gesture, as he pinned the spray into my buttonhole, as though he too had found a kind of magic in our afternoon walk through the woods, and wanted me to have something to remind me of the pleasant hours we had spent together.

Now, I sighed, as I picked up the cone, this souvenir would bring memories more bitter than sweet, for I would see the gift as a mere trick in the art of gaining my confidence, to find out more about me for his professional purposes as a security man.

I opened the top drawer and dropped the twig beside my make-up kit, not wanting to throw it away, yet wondering what pleasure such a souvenir would give me should I keep it.

With another sigh, I removed my fox fur hat. It was a relief to be free of the tightness of the hat band, and of the very weight of the hat on my crown. I had longed to take it off in the café when I was talking to Karl, but I did not dare do so, for I knew that my hair would have been moulded to my head like an unsightly bathing cap, after being enclosed in the hot, close-fitting fur for almost eight hours. Neither Karl nor Phil would have thought me at all glamorous had they seen me as the mirror at present reflected me back!

Apart from the fact that my hair was a mess, I looked tired and down-at-the-mouth. Even my eyes, whose hyacinth blueness had reminded Karl of his mother's, had lost their usual sparkle.

I was peering into the mirror, wishing there was some way in which I could transform myself into someone as glamorous looking as Sula Neilson, who never seemed to have a hair out of place or a smudged lipstick line, when I noticed a red light flashing on the bedside table, the signal that there was a message for me.

Wondering who wanted to get in touch with me, I telephoned the desk and was told to get in touch with Mrs. Mabel Angus in room number 1117.

I telephoned Mabel's room immediately, and

she replied briskly, "So you are in at last, Miranda! We have been trying to get in touch with you for ages! What on earth have you found to do with yourself all day? You weren't at any of the meetings," she went on reproachfully.

"It's a long story," I began.

"In that case," interrupted Mabel, "save it for this evening! A crowd of us, including your friend Phil Hunter and the Neilsons, have arranged to go to a Weinkeller near the Akademie der Wissenschaften in the old quarter for dinner, at about nine o'clock, and I was hoping we would be able to persuade you to join us."

As if by magic my tiredness and my incipient fit of the blues vanished. I was not going to have to spend the evening on my own after all. Not only that, Mabel seemed to be anxious that I join the party, and not just as if she was asking me because she thought she ought to.

"That sounds wonderful!" I breathed a happy sigh. "I should love to come with you! Phil Hunter suggested earlier that I meet him and the Neilsons in the cocktail bar in the gallery, but he didn't mention anything about a meal to follow."

"We arranged about the meal only an hour ago, when we bumped into Hunter and Sir Jack in the elevator. Incidentally," she sighed, "I think that my Maurizio finds Sula very attractive. Thank goodness she has Phil to occupy her attention!"

"From the look in your Maurizio's eyes when he gazes at you, I don't think you need worry about Sula!" I assured her.

Mabel laughed, and when she replied there was a pleased tone in her voice. "Maurizio and I have known each other for a very long time. We first met at a conference about seven years ago, and have met annually ever since, though in between times, I doubt if we even think of each other! We enjoy each other's company for the week, and that is that. It is a very pleasant and useful arrangement."

"I am sure it is!" I agreed, smiling to myself.

"By the way," Mabel went on, "we are not going to dress up for dinner tonight. If the weather clears, we shall walk to the Kavalierkeller. It is quite near the hotel, and it is rather pleasant to wander through the old quarter of the city by night. *Molto romantico*, as Maurizio would say!" she laughed.

For a moment my blues returned. It would be "*molto romantico*" for Mabel and her Maurizio, and for Sula with Phil, but what about me? No doubt I would be left to make polite conversation with Sir Jack Neilson, Sula's father, while the others strolled happily arm in arm along the narrow, dimly lit alleys!

Still, I decided firmly, as I stripped off my clothes and went into the bathroom for a shower and to wash my limp and lackluster hair, Sir Jack was an amusing conversationalist, as I had learned on previous occasions when we had talked together, and it would be much more fun wining and dining in a typical Viennese Keller, than sitting alone in my room, reading a guidebook!

As I dried my hair I listened to a selection of

Strauss waltzes on the radio and wishfully imagined myself back in the Rathaus, dancing in Phil Hunter's arms to these very tunes.

However, when the orchestra played the opening bars of "Tales from the Vienna Woods," my mood changed again, for I remembered that Phil had no romantic yearning for me, as I had for him. I was a girl he had asked out so that he could vet me for his special security reasons, not because he found me at all attractive, and no doubt the only reason which would make him seek out my company again was that he had seen me on my own with Karl Lippe in the coffee room—a fact which might reawaken his suspicions of me!

I wondered if there would be more subtle questioning in store for me during the evening ahead, and I mischievously decided that I would do a little leg pulling, a decision which, as it happened, I did not put into practice, although I spent the next hour amusing myself by thinking up some outrageous things I could hint at when we talked together!

My hair is very thick and longish, and in spite of making use of the hairdryer I had brought with me, it took considerably longer to dry than I had allowed for. As a result, I arrived for our meeting at the cocktail bar a quarter of an hour behind the time Phil had indicated he would expect to see me.

Because of the inclement weather, most of the guests who were staying in the Mahler had decided not to venture forth that evening, with the result that the hotel bars, cafés and restaurants were filled to overflowing, and the cocktail bar on the gallery overlooking the dining room was no exception. It was so crowded, in fact, that to begin with, I could not see any of my friends. However, Phil, who had been looking out for me, saw me standing, hesitant, under the archway which led into the gallery, and came pushing his way past the small groups of chattering people to reach my side.

"I thought you had got lost, or at very least fallen asleep after your exercise this afternoon!" he smiled down at me, and taking me by the elbow he steered me to the far corner of the bar counter, where Sula, Mabel, and the others were already ensconced.

I smiled and said good evening to the people I recognized as I squeezed past them, and much to my amusement, I noticed Aldo Giovane, the dress designer, deep in conversation with Karl Lippe. I had no doubts, seeing the smile which twitched at the corners of Phil's mouth as he glanced at them, that he was the one who had arranged their introduction.

Aldo was looking happy and gesticulated freely with his long-fingered, softly smooth hands, but poor Karl looked ill at ease, and his shadow, Major Dietrich, who was talking to the attractive countrywoman who had been in their party at the opening reception, made no attempt to rescue him from Aldo, as he would have done if it had been to me that Karl was talking.

Karl cast me an expressive glance as I insinuated my way between the table where he was seated and the bar counter, to the tall bar stool

to his right, which Sir Jack Neilson had been re-
serving for me. When I clambered onto it, Phil
came to stand immediately behind me, hiding
Aldo and his new friend from my view.

"What happened to you, Miranda?" Sula
asked me. "Father declared you must have been
kidnapped by one of your admirers, but Phil
said you had probably fallen asleep after an
overdose of fresh Vienna Woods air, combined
with a surfeit of rich Viennese cream cakes!"

She gave me a questioning glance.

"Is it true that you had another round of
coffee and cakes after we parted company?"

"I am adapting to the Viennese way of life
very quickly!" I replied with a smile. "It is a
way of life I can enjoy, for a week at least!"

"What do you want to drink, Miranda?" asked
Sir Jack, signaling to the barman for attention.

"Miranda is an 'achtel Gespritzt' drinker, so
she tells me!" Phil's eyes twinkled at me.

"A what?" Sula gave a squeak of laughter.

" 'Achtel Gespritzt'!" repeated Phil. "White
wine and soda water," he explained.

"Oh!" Sula giggled again. "I thought at first
you had said 'Alka Seltzer'!"

"As a matter of fact," I turned to Sir Jack, "I
would like a glass of white wine—but without
the soda, please."

As I waited for the wine to be brought to me,
I glanced around the party. Arnold Weissman
was standing beside Maurizio Lenno, behind
Sula and Mabel, who, like me were seated on bar
stools, but I could not see Senga Watson.

"Isn't Senga joining us tonight?" I asked in surprise.

"She should be here any minute," replied Mabel. "Marguerite Dupont telephoned just as we were leaving our room. It was something to do with Ivy Sikorska, I gathered," she shrugged. "I suppose, as senior female British representative now that poor Dorinda is out of action, Senga will be expected to help with anything that crops up about Ivy. Funeral arrangements and the like, you know. Ivy had no next-of-kin, and apparently no close friend apart from Dorinda, to attend to these matters."

"That is hard luck on Senga!" I exclaimed.

"I don't think it will worry her. She is a very efficient person, and likes being helpful."

"Speak of the devil!" observed Arnold Weissman. "Here she comes now!"

As I had done minutes earlier, Senga Watson hesitated under the high arched entrance to the cocktail bar, looking hopefully around to see if she could spot us.

Arnold pulled a large white handkerchief from his pocket and waved it high in the air to attract her attention.

She spotted his gesture and waved gaily back before she began to maneuver her way past the closely packed tables towards us.

She looked flushed and excited, and I wondered if she had been afraid of missing us, for it was now almost nine o'clock, but her excitement was due to something much more dramatic than the thought of missing out on a dinner date.

"You will never guess the latest!" she exclaimed as she breathlessly struggled onto the stool which Arnold had kept vacant for her. "I can hardly believe it myself!"

"Believe what?" asked Mabel.

"I shall have a drink first—a brandy!" she decided. "I really need one, after what I have heard!"

"What have you heard?" queried Phil, frowning. "What has been happening that you are so tensed up?"

Senga sipped her drink slowly before she answered him.

"I'm surprised your friends in the police here didn't tell you," she gave him a curious glance. "It's about Ivy Sikorska," she went on. "The medical authorities have announced the result of their post-mortem, and—" she hesitated and looked at each of us in turn. "You won't believe this any more than I could, but Ivy didn't die of a heart attack. She died—" Her voice shook, and she took another sip of her drink and nervously licked her lips before adding the news which stunned us all to a momentary silence. "She died of an overdose of sleeping pills!"

I shivered involuntarily, and I was not the only one who was affected by Senga's dramatic pronouncement. Mabel was so startled that she set her glass of sherry down on the counter with a noisy bang, and even Sula, who had never met Ivy, looked quite shocked.

Phil was the first to break the silence.

"Do the authorities think she took a deliberate overdose, or was it accidental?" he demanded sharply.

Senga shrugged.

"It was Madame Dupont who broke the news to me. She also said that in view of the fact Ivy was a stranger here, and attending an international conference, etc., étc., they are going to give her the benefit of the doubt. An accidental death does not seem so nasty as suicide. Moreover, the post-mortem showed what we all knew, that Ivy had consumed a considerable amount of alcohol shortly before her death, and it has been agreed that the poor soul was so tipsy when she was taking her pills before going to bed that she did not know what she was doing, and took too many."

"How awful!" I shuddered. "The poor woman! But you would have thought all that wine she took would have made her so sleepy she wouldn't have needed to take a sleeping pill ..." my voice trailed off.

"We'll not ask ourselves questions," said Senga decisively. "If the authorities are content with an accidental death verdict, that's it."

"But what if it wasn't an accident?" Mabel blurted out. "What if it was suicide!" She bit her lip. "People don't take their own lives for a joke! Something sends them over the edge of despair. Loneliness. The feeling of being unwanted by anyone. And I feel guilty!" she went on harshly. "Ivy was a pest and a hanger-on, as we all knew, and we all did our best to avoid her, but since her death I have thought a lot about her, thinking how lonely she must have been, even in a crowded conference room.

"We have our families, our friends, our colleagues. Most of us have a job outside the home and meet people, but Ivy had nobody. Writing was all she had, and as we all know, writing, at the best of times, is a very lonely business."

Throughout Mabel's discourse I had sat silent, trying to remember something about the telephone call I had received from Ivy only an hour or so before her death.

Up till now, I had made a determined effort to forget about the call, firstly because I did not want to think of Ivy's tragic death, and secondly because the call had been such a rambling one that I had not thought it worth remembering.

Now, however, as I tried to bring it back to mind, I could remember some of the conversation, and it was this talk of an overdose which was niggling my memory, for there was something about it which didn't seem right. Senga had mentioned sleeping pills—sleeping pills—my voice shakily repeated the words under my breath.

"That's it!" I spoke aloud now, and my unexpected interjection, high-pitched with excitement, made everyone who was close to me turn to look at me.

"I knew there was something odd about what you were telling us, Senga!" I stared at the older woman. "It was the bit about sleeping pills! Ivy could not have taken an overdose of them, because she never took such things!"

"What do you mean?" gasped Mabel. "How can you be so positive about that? Why, you only met Ivy for the first time when you arrived here, and I don't see her discussing what pills she took with a stranger!"

Phil looked at me with his keen scrutiny and put in a question.

"What made you say that Mrs. Sikorska didn't take sleeping pills, Miranda? Have you definite knowledge that she didn't, or were you merely going by something she mentioned casually, and which may not have been true?"

"I know that Ivy did not take anything like that, because she told me so, very firmly!" I looked around the circle of startled faces. "She told me so," I repeated slowly, "on the very night she died, or more accurately, the morning she died, because it was at one o'clock in the morning, an hour before her death, that she telephoned to my room to speak to me!"

"Miranda! What on earth are you talking about!" gasped Mabel. "This is the first time you have mentioned a telephone call from Ivy that night!"

"I know," I agreed. "There seemed no point in mentioning it before. Ivy was dead, and the call she had made to me was so fuddled, it didn't seem worth talking about. I mean," I glanced around them for understanding, "we all knew she had had rather a lot to drink, and the story she told me was so absurd, it merely confirmed that. She really quite wandered. I didn't want to remember her like that. In any case," I went on, "it isn't even as if I was the last person she spoke to. As you all know, she telephoned Dorinda much later—and talking of Dorinda, no doubt, knowing Ivy for so many years she will be able to confirm what I have said about her not taking sleeping pills."

"Miranda! Please!" Phil put a hand on my arm. "You have gone off at a tangent. What we want to know is, why did Mrs. Sikorska talk to you about sleeping pills that night? Do you think she was trying to cover up her future action, or something like that?"

I shook my head.

"I was the one who mentioned sleeping pills first," I said. "As I have been telling you, she seemed somewhat hysterical and overexcited, and there was this impossible story she kept on about. She insisted that she had just seen her husband in the flesh!

"I told her to calm down and take a sleeping pill, and have a good night's rest, and everything would be all right in the morning.

"She was most indignant at this suggestion." I stopped, and it was at Phil, rather than at the others I looked. "You know, I have forgotten other bits of the conversation at the moment, but her answer to that remark I remember with extraordinary clarity. Ivy said quite distinctly, 'I have never taken a sleeping pill or a tranquilizer in my life. Even when I heard the news of poor Jan's death, I refused the offer of one, and I am certainly not going to take one now that I have found out that he is still alive!'"

Phil looked at me thoughtfully.

"That sounds very definite, Miranda. I wonder if we could get Dorinda Grey to confirm what you have said?"

Senga shook her head. "After she had told me

125

about Ivy, I asked Madame Dupont for the latest news about Dorinda, and she told me that she had had a relapse, and must under no circumstances be disturbed for the next few days. It seemed that the police had already asked if they could interrogate her about her friend, and had been told that it was out of the question meantime."

"I think you should have a word with the police yourself, Miranda," Phil advised me. "One of the officers at headquarters is a friend of mine. I shall go with you to see him, if you like. The sooner you tell them what you have told us, the better!"

"It doesn't make sense, though, does it?" I shook my head. "Why did she tell me she didn't take sleeping pills, if she had a bottle of them to hand?"

Before Phil could reply, Mabel offered. "Perhaps at the back of her mind, Ivy knew that one day she might do what she did that night, but didn't want to admit it to herself. Moreover, she was a very excitable and highly strung woman, and the shock of thinking she had seen her husband alive after all that time must have sent her over the top!"

"I should imagine that anyone would get a shock if someone they thought was dead walked back into her life!" said Sula. "Incidentally," she added curiously, "what made her so sure that it was her husband she saw?"

"I don't think she could have made a positive identification, after all that time! Do you think she saw him as he was, thirty years ago, and forgot the passage of time?"

"Why thirty years?" asked Sula.

"Jan Sikorski, Ivy's husband, was killed in a raid over Berlin, and that is all of thirty years or more ago. He would be an old man now!"

"Less of the old man!" protested Sir Jack. "I was in that war too, remember, and I don't think of myself as old!"

"Well, he would look thirty years older, and people do change in that time," replied Senga.

"She seemed very sure it was he," I remarked. "She told me something about him—some mannerism he had, at least I think that is what she said, that confirmed her recognition. I have forgotten éxactly what it was, for the moment, although I daresay I could bring it to mind if I had to. The truth is, I was not paying a great deal of attention to her maunderings on the telephone that night. She sounded a trifle tipsy, I was tired and wanted to get to bed, and it was at that point, when she was describing the man, I suggested she take a sleeping pill and have a good night's sleep and she would be able to think straighter in the morning."

"And this is where I suggest that you come with me to see my friend at headquarters," interrupted Phil, and he took a firm hold on my arm.

"We shall meet up with you at the Kavalier-keller in about an hour," he said to the others. "We shouldn't be any longer than that."

"For goodness' sake, Phil!" Sula exclaimed indignantly. "There is no need to spoil our evening

127

because some silly old creature was so fuddled she took an overdose! It has nothing to do with you, anyway." She glared at me, as if she had thought I wanted to take Phil away from her. "If Miranda wants to make a song and dance about this question of sleeping pills, it is up to her to contact the police. She doesn't need you to go along and hold her hand!" she groused.

"Why not telephone your friend, Phil?" suggested Sir Jack. "Tell him what Miranda has just told us, and ask him what he thinks should be done."

Phil hesitated. He looked from Sula, whose stormy-eyed expression betrayed her annoyance at the thought of being deprived of his company for an hour or so, to her father, and finally to me.

"Very well," he said eventually. "I suppose that is the sensible thing to do, so if you will excuse me," he set his glass on the counter, "I shall go and phone Werner right away."

He hurried off, to return some ten minutes later with the information that the police did not think it necessary to interview me. They were quite satisfied that Ivy, as Mabel had already conjectured, hadn't been telling me the truth, because the medicine bottle they had taken from her room still contained one of the pills whose traces had been found in her body.

Moreover, the bottle, which had her name, the address of a chemist in her home town, the written advice not to exceed the stated dose, and the given dose printed on its label, also had a date on it, and the date when the prescription had been handed out was a mere two days before Ivy had left for Vienna, which indicated that the bottle must have been almost full the night she took the overdose of its contents.

"So that is that," Phil finished, telling us of his conversation with the police. "The authorities are satisfied as to the cause of death. They don't want things stirred up unnecessarily, and they are willing to give Ivy the benefit of the 'death by misadventure' verdict to save any unpleasantness."

I only half-listened to what he was saying, for snippets of memory about the dead woman's conversation with me were returning.

"It's odd," I mused more to myself than the others, "although for the moment I cannot recall exactly what peculiarity of gesture or expression or distinguishing mark confirmed in Ivy's maudlin mind that the man she bumped into in the elevator was her husband, on the evening after her death, at the reception which we all attended, something I noticed momentarily recalled the conversation I had with her, but again," I shook my head, "I can't remember what it was!" I pursed my lips in exasperation.

Sula, who had not quite got over her huff, said crossly, "Come off it, Miranda! You are letting your novelist's imagination work overtime. As for you, Phil," she snapped at her companion, "the trouble with you is that your job makes you suspect everyone and everything. It makes life very difficult for your friends at times!"

With that, she peremptorily held out her hands to him, so that he could help her down from the high stool on which she was sitting, and this was the signal for the rest of the party to finish their drinks and follow Sula and Phil from the cocktail bar.

Chapter Ten

We made our way through the crowded cocktail bar to the narrow stairway which led down to the dining room, and through it to the reception hall beyond.

As I had guessed we might, we paired off into couples, with Sir Jack, Sula's father, accompanying me, and chatting pleasantly about my previous visit to Vienna.

While Arnold Weissman went out to the hotel porch to find out what the weather was like, to decide if we should walk to our destination or if he should ask the doorman to hail a couple of taxis to take us the short distance to the Weinkeller, Sir Jack took the coat I had been carrying and held it up for me to put on.

While I was buttoning it up, Sula draped her long black fox fur coat around her and pulled the attached hood over her hair so that it framed her face, accentuating the creamy softness of her skin and the perfection of her lovely features.

I noticed the sideways glance that Maurizio Lenno flickered in her direction, and he was not the only man who was attracted by her beauty, for every male who was in the vicinity was casting surreptitious looks in her direction.

Phil Hunter caught my glance as I turned my attention from his companion to listen to a remark Sir Jack had made to me, and he smiled pleasantly at me. If I hadn't been convinced that his interest in me was largely impersonal, I would have sworn that he gave me a quick wink, almost as if he was reminding me of my remark earlier that day about Sula and her sister models—that it was the face of the girl, and not the clothes she wore, which attracted a man's attention to a girl.

"Look! Arnold is signaling us to go out!" Sir Jack took my arm and urged me towards the door. "I don't know if he means he has ordered the taxis, or if he is merely indicating that it is dry outside now and we can start walking."

We walked through the swing doors of the comfortably heated hotel, and as we stepped outside the biting coldness of the night air brought the sting of tears to my eyes. In spite of my cosy coat, I shivered perceptibly.

"Haven't you a scarf or something to put over your head?" asked Sir Jack solicitously.

"I didn't realize it would be as cold as this!" I shivered again.

He held me back from catching up to the others, who had left in front of us.

"I think you should go back up to your room and get a hat or something," he advised. "You mustn't catch a chill, or you might miss the grand ball the government is laying on for us the night after tomorrow!"

My ears were now so cold that they ached with pain, and I realized it would be foolhardy not to do as he suggested, even if by wearing a head covering I would flatten the hairdo I had spent over an hour arranging.

Mabel and Senga had wisely tied scarves over their heads and all of the men sported ear-muffling hats, and as a fresh blast of icy wind sent a further stab of pain through my eardrums I appreciated why there were so many hat shops, with fur hats abounding, for both men and women in this lovely but winter-cold Austrian capital city.

"You are quite right, Sir Jack," I agreed. "I shall go back to my room to get something to put over my head. If you tell me how to get to the Kavalierkeller, I shall meet up with you all there."

"Nonsense, my dear!" said Sir Jack firmly. "The others can go on ahead and get a table. I shall come back to the Mahler with you, and wait for you by the elevator."

He called to Mabel and Maurizio, who were a couple of strides ahead of us, to say that we were returning to the hotel but would rejoin the party at the Weinkeller later.

Phil looked around as he heard Sir Jack call to the other couple, and in the light of the street lamps which illuminated the road along which we were walking, I detected a puzzled frown on his face. He stopped, as if he wanted to find out what was wrong, but Sula tugged impatiently at his arm, and with another puzzled backward glance he moved ahead again.

Sir Jack and I reentered the Mahler, and I

left him to wait for me in the elevator hall while I went up to my room.

I stood hesitant beside the dressing table, wondering if I should put on my fur hat, or if a silk scarf would give me sufficient protection against the cold. After a couple of minutes I reluctantly decided that common sense should prevail, and that I could count the time I had spent setting my hair as wasted, so I firmly pulled my cosy fox hat down over my ears and hurried back to the elevator.

When I emerged from the elevator at the ground floor, Sir Jack was standing near the reception desk a few yards away, talking to Aldo Giovane. As he caught sight of me, a fleeting expression of relief crossed his face, and as I approached him he turned to me and said briskly, "There you are, my dear! I was just telling Aldo that you and I were going to join Sula and your other friends for dinner in the Kavalierkeller."

"Sula is being very naughty!" simpered Aldo. "She would not tell me what she was going to do this evening. She knew I wanted all my girls tucked up in bed early tonight so that they will be fresh and lovely for tomorrow's show, but she is so headstrong, and she took advantage of the fact that I was talking to that handsome young man Mr. Hunter introduced me to, to slip away from me!

"By the time I made my apologies, and managed to get away from Herr Lippe, you had all disappeared. However, when I was on my way to ask the doorman if he had seen you, I noticed Sir Jack by the elevator, and he tells me you are on your way to the Kavalierkeller?" He looked at me hopefully.

Short of being downright rude, it was plain that we would have to ask him to join us, and Aldo accepted Sir Jack's invitation to do so with alacrity.

"I'll have to get my coat from the cloakroom," he told us. "I shan't be a minute!" He flashed a smile of thanks to us as he hurried across the hall.

"Sula is not going to be pleased about this!" sighed her father. "When Aldo is around, no one else gets much chance to speak, and Sula likes to be the center of attention, I'm afraid!"

"It's food, not conversation, I am interested in at the moment!" I replied cheerfully. "I am quite sure there must be something in the air of Vienna which whets my appetite!"

"It is the Viennese cooking that does it!" smiled Sir Jack. "I believe this place we are going to tonight has a reputation for serving the best Hungarian dishes in town, which is saying something!"

We strolled towards the swing doors, and as we neared the exit, Aldo, who was wearing a magnificent fur-collared coat and cossack-style fur hat, which many a woman would have envied, came hurrying after us.

He minced along by our side, chattering nonstop as we crossed the Wollzeile to enter the Postgasse.

Sir Jack stopped as we reached the corner of the Bäckerstrasse, which was less brightly lit than the main road which we had left, and where there was still quite a lot of snow and slush piled along the gutters.

"I can't remember if Sula said to turn left along this street or go straight on. Can you remember, Miranda?" he turned to me.

"I think we turn left here. As I remember, the Kavalierkeller is not far from the old university," I told him. "In any case, we can't get lost. It is either up this street or the next one, and we can always ask directions from someone."

We turned left along the narrow alleyway, with its old houses, some of which dated back as far as the sixteenth century. They looked strangely dark and forbidding this dark and gloomy night, and the dim lamplight only served to emphasize the disturbing loneliness of this quiet lane.

"Isn't it spooky, my dears!" Aldo moved closer to us. "All very Third Man, and all that."

It was rather spooky, I agreed with a shiver, and it wasn't only because the rising wind sent strange moans and forlorn screams echoing under the ancient eaves. It was because at this moment I had a peculiar sensation of isolation, as if Sir Jack and Aldo and I were the only beings alive in the neighborhood. The black crows that circled over the rooftops by day had long since returned to their rookeries. The townsfolk had retreated to the comfort of their firesides. Not a solitary bat with high-pitched screech wheeled down on us, and even the noise of the traffic from the main road we had left only seconds earlier was muffled by the tall, narrow buildings which bordered the alley.

"This doesn't seem to me to be the kind of street in which one would find a well-known Weinkeller," moaned Aldo peevishly. "I am sure we have taken the wrong turning."

"No, no! We are heading in the right direction," I replied, as the lane opened out into a small square. "That is the old university over there, now the Academy of Sciences, and if we go on past the Jesuit Church at the corner and turn left we should reach the Kavalierkeller in a few minutes."

"I hope you are right," he sniffed. "It is beginning to snow again, and I don't want to get soaked." He glanced around and added with a pout, "There isn't even a taxi in sight!"

"I doubt if any taxicab driver would loiter here in the hope of a fare," replied Sir Jačk, taking an even firmer grip on my arm as if he too was being made as uneasy as I was by the disquieting silence of the faintly lit square.

We turned into the romantically named Schönlaterngasse—the Alley of the Beautiful Lanterns—and here we saw the first people we had encountered on our walk to the Keller. A man, his coat collar turned up to muffle his face from the biting wind and with a black homburg hat pulled well down over his ears, was standing at the corner talking to a man astride a motorbike, gesturing with his hand as if giving directions.

As we walked past them, the driver kicked the starter and the powerful engine of his bike roared into life. The noise echoed and reechoed back from the gloomy houses on either side.

At this part the pavement was too narrow to walk two abreast and Sir Jack released his grip of my arm, letting Aldo mince along in front of me while he followed behind, picking his way as carefully as I was doing, for the slush and dampness on the pavement was freezing over, making walking a slippery and precarious business.

"Ah! Good!" exclaimed Sir Jack, tapping me on the shoulder. "There is the Kavalierkeller over there!" He indicated a dimly lit signboard which creaked gratingly as the wrought-iron angle on which it hung swayed to and fro in the blustering wind.

Aldo Giovane, anxious to get under cover from the thickening snowflakes as quickly as possible, darted across the road, as light and agile on his feet as a prima ballerina, while Sir Jack followed at a more sedate and careful pace.

I hesitated at the edge of the pavement, less eager than they had been to plough my way through the ankle-deep slush of the gutter at this particular point, and I looked along the road to see if there was a better place to traverse the street. I noticed that there was no slush over a drain grating about a couple of yards further on, and decided to make my crossing from this point. As I walked towards it, behind me I could hear the noisy overrevving of the motorbike. I glanced around, but the driver had not switched on his lights, and since there was no other traffic in this one-way street, I stepped over the drain and onto the road.

Without warning, without even switching on his lights, the motorcyclist unexpectedly took off and came speeding along the slippery road right at me.

As the powerful machine came hurtling towards me, Sir Jack shouted an angry warning.

I tried to get out of its path, but the road was so icy, the rubber soles of my boots could not get a good grip on the surface, and in my haste I slithered to my knees, letting out a scream of fright as I realized I would not get out of the way of the bike before it was on me, and certain that in another second I was going to be catapulted into eternity.

At my yell the driver switched on his headlight, which pinpointed me in its glare. Instead of trying to swerve around me, he braked, a false move which made the machine skid sideways and come slithering towards me, broadside on.

As I wildly tried to scramble to my feet, my arm was grabbed by fingers with the strength of steel, and I was jerked across the road and miraculously out of harm's way, by the bold, swift action of a man who until this moment I had dismissed as an amusing but lightweight and self-centered young fop—Aldo Giovane, the dress designer.

Aldo held me firmly until he was satisfied that my legs would support me once more, while Sir Jack shook his fist after the man on the machine who, having gained control of the bike, and apparently satisfied that I had not been hurt, had gone speeding off around the corner.

"Careless brute!" growled Sir Jack. "I don't know how he missed seeing you cross the road, even without his headlight on. You were directly under a light standard!"

"From the look of him, all that bulky leather gear and studding, I should imagine he is one of those layabouts who make a game of frightening people on their bikes!"

I could not reconcile Aldo's prim, light-toned voice with his recent bold reaction to my danger, or with the steely grip of the fingers which had pulled me to safety.

"Somehow I did not imagine such things happened in Vienna," he went on. "But I have seen youngsters play this silly game in Amsterdam and Hamburg, although," he shrugged, "usually they tend to play the game in groups."

"Aldo!" I looked at him with respect. "That was a very brave action. You saved my life. What can I say to express my thanks?"

He gave a silly giggle, but the gleam in his eyes was more mischievous than inane as he replied, "My dear! How could I possibly have stood by and watched that elegant coat of yours being dragged to shreds?" He waved his hands in one of his typical gestures. "And speaking of clothes," he went on before I could say anything, "since I don't want this coat of mine to get any wetter, do let us get down to the Keller before we are transformed into snowmen!"

With that, he swaggered ahead of us to an opening in the iron railing which bordered the building we were approaching. From here, a very steep flight of stone steps led down to a small flagged courtyard and a basement room, through whose open door we could hear the sound of voices and music and smell the appetizing aroma of hot food and wine.

Sir Jack shook his head and looked at me as we prepared to follow Aldo.

"That was amazing!" he said. "Quite amazing! That man thought and moved with the speed of lightning just now. I had let out a cry, thinking you hadn't a chance, but before the sound of my exclamation died, there he was, dragging you out of harm's way!"

He shook his head once more. "I can still hardly credit it! Aldo Giovane, of all people, to act like that! I take back everything I have thought or said about him, and what is more," he whispered as he followed me down the steep, snow-slippery steps to the cellar, "I shall never again judge a man by his outward appearance!

"Mark you, Miranda," he continued, "Sula did tell me, when I made a stupid joke about her employer, that there was much more to Aldo than met the eye. She said I must not let myself be deceived by his odd ways, but knowing her I thought she was merely being loyal to the man for whom she was working."

Aldo, who had negotiated the stairway with more speed than we had dared, stood waiting impatiently for us in the tiny flagged yard, beside the door which led into the Weinkeller.

When we reached his side he signed to Sir Jack to lead the way through the high, arched doorway which led into a long vaulted room so dimly lit that it was impossible to see upwards to the ceiling. There were three long refectory-type tables set in line down the middle of the room, and the guttering light from the candles which stood on them cast strange, malevolent expressions on the faces of the diners who sat there.

Along three walls of the vault, bench tables and seats with high wooden backs gave the appearance of a sideless, old-fashioned train coach, the way they were set back to back giving a certain degree of privacy to the people who sat in the small compartments.

The fourth side of the room, to the left of the doorway, was taken up by a long bar, the front part of whose wooden counter was carved out to look like rustic fencing, through which bunches of wooden grapes, vine tendrils, and finely fashioned vine leaves peeped out.

Sir Jack lingered just inside the entrance, peering through the gloom to look for his daughter and her party, and I was glad of the few moments of respite this gave me before meeting up with them, for I was still feeling shaken after my near-accident and I wanted to pull myself together before we rejoined them.

"There they are, over there!" piped Aldo. "Look! Where the man in the gypsy costume is fiddling away in Sula's ear!"

Sir Jack moved forward to the table indicated, and Aldo followed behind me, muttering, "I do hope there is going to be enough room for all of us at that table. It doesn't look as if there will be, and I do hate being crushed against people."

"What on earth kept you so long?" demanded Sula as we reached the table. "I am absolutely starving, but Phil would not allow any of us to order until you arrived!"

"You can put the blame on me, Sula, darling," said Aldo, moving forward and insinuating himself between the refectory table and the wooden bench seat to sit beside Maurizio and facing his model. "When your father very kindly asked me if I would care to join your little party, I had to go and get my coat and hat from the cloakroom, and you know how slow the attendant there is, especially where I am concerned," he sniffed. "He never seems to notice me!"

"I am surprised you came along here," said Sula. "I was quite sure you would be dining at the hotel with Karl Lippe. You seemed to be getting along so well in the cocktail bar when we left."

Aldo grimaced. "That young man is not my type," he observed. "I found him very heavy going. He simply has no sense of humor! Life is very real and very earnest with him, and what's more, Sula, he gave me the impression that he didn't quite approve of me, or of what I do. It was rather off-putting!"

"I wouldn't take young Lippe's opinion into consideration if I were you, Aldo." Sir Jack smiled at him, as he stood waiting for me to take my seat beside Aldo and opposite Phil, while a waiter brought a chair so that he could sit at the head of the table, facing down past the four side bench seats. "Miranda and I both think very highly of you, and always will, as you must know."

The warmth in her father's voice as he addressed the young designer made Sula give him a surprised look. She looked even more surprised as her father continued.

"Not two minutes ago, at considerable risk to himself, Aldo managed to save Miranda from what could have been a very, very nasty accident!"

Sula gaped, and Phil leaned across the table to stare at me as he rapped out, "Why, what happened?"

"It was nothing," Aldo interrupted quickly. "Just a bit of quick thinking."

"A bit of quick thinking, and what was more important, a bit of damned brave acting!" said Sir Jack. "You know, I don't think I have ever seen anyone move so quickly over the ground since the Montreal Olympics!"

"You can put my speed of movement down to my ballet training," Aldo smiled his mischievous smile. "You have no idea how invaluable I have found that training for so many things! It certainly helped me gain my foils championship!"

"Yes," nodded Sir Jack, "that I could understand! You have to be fast and light on the feet for that."

Phil interrupted him impatiently. "You still haven't told us what happened!" he said harshly.

"We were crossing the road to reach this place," said Sir Jack. "Miranda was trailing behind, because the surface was very slippery. She was about halfway across when a motorbike, without any lights, came speeding down the road straight towards her.

"She yelled as she struggled to get out of its way, and we turned around to see what was happening. The driver foolishly braked too hard, and came skidding broadside towards her. Miranda slipped as she made a desperate attempt to jump clear, and fell on her knees, and as she did so Aldo darted to her rescue and pulled her out of harm's way just in time. They both missed being bowled over by a hair's breadth!"

"What about the motorcyclist?" demanded Phil in an angry voice. "What happened to him?"

Sir Jack inhaled an angry breath, and his lips tightened to a fine line.

"He got the bike under control and went speeding off out of sight around the corner, without stopping to apologize for the accident his carelessness had almost caused, or for the fright he had given Miranda! Young boors like that should not be allowed a license!" he added with indignation. "He was damned lucky not to be facing a manslaughter charge, which he might well have done if Aldo hadn't acted so courageously!"

Aldo uttered a self-conscious laugh.

"Thinking back to what happened, I don't feel quite so courageous now!" he muttered shakily. "In fact, I feel quite weak at the knees, and could do with a glass of slivovitz to stiffen them up again!"

"I am sure you could, too, Miranda," he turned to me with a friendly smile. "Even in this light, you look a bit pale about the gills!"

Chapter Eleven

Sir Jack signaled the wine waiter and gave him our order, while I studied the menu card which Sula had handed to me. I was hoping that no further reference would be made to my near-accident, because I felt shivery with nerves when I thought back to it, but Phil insisted on being told exactly what had happened outside the Weinkeller. When I reluctantly repeated the tale, he interrupted me with questions when he thought I had glossed over some detail.

"For goodness' sake, Phil!" I was grateful to Sula for interrupting our conversation. "Leave Miranda be! You are always wanting to make mountains out of molehills! In a minute you will be telling us that someone deliberately tried to run Miranda down!"

She turned to me. "Don't pay any attention to him." She shook her head. "Have a look at the menu and choose what you want from it. I don't know about you, but I am starving. I'll pass out if I don't get something to eat soon."

Aldo gave her a peevish glance.

"Darling Sula!" he exclaimed. "Ten years from now, you are going to be fat and podgy with multiple chins, and nobody, but nobody will employ you as a model!"

"Of course they will!" she retorted airily, signaling to the waiter to indicate that we were ready to give our order. "There are more overweight women than any other kind, so there will always be a demand for pretty, plump models to show off clothes to them. In fact," she ran her hands over her slim hips, "there are very few women as pencil-thin as I am. In any case, what does it matter what I look like in future," she turned to the man who was sitting beside her, flickering her long lashes at him with exaggerated coyness. "You will still love me when I am fat and forty, won't you, darling?"

Phil grinned.

"I daresay I shall, Sula! After all, I loved you when you were a fat and chubby six-year-old, with a temper to match your hair." He gave me a quick wink as he was speaking. "So if I have managed to put up with you for seventeen years, no doubt I shall be able to do the same for another seventeen."

I made a rapid calculation and decided that Sula must therefore be about the same age as myself, although in sophistication and self-assurance she made me seem much younger.

"Well, Miranda?" Sir Jack addressed me. "Have you decided what you want to eat?"

"I'm having the paprika steaks," said Sula. "They serve them with a superb potato concoction, courgettes and red peppers, and a heavenly sauce!"

"I haven't made up my mind yet," I spoke

hesitantly. There were still a few butterflies fluttering around in my stomach, and the thought
of food was repugnant at this moment, but I did
not want to spoil the evening for the others by
ordering nothing.

"How about the veal dish we both enjoyed at
the Kahlenberg?" Phil suggested. "That's what
I am going to order, with a side salad."

"Yes, that would be nice," I nodded, my spirits rising at the idea that Phil had remembered
our first meal together.

The evening passed pleasantly, with Aldo and
Sula discussing the fashion show that was being
put on the following day, while the others talked
about their conferences, and people they had
met. I sat, for the most part silent, but quite
content to be here among friends, in the
pleasant atmosphere of the old Weinkeller, looking across at Phil Hunter whom I found so attractive and occasionally answering questions he
put to me with a nod of my head.

When we left the Weinkeller it was Phil who
took my arm as we strolled back to the Mahler
along the quiet streets whose snow-covered
pavements muffled the sound of our footsteps,
although our voices, and particularly Sula's in-
fectious giggle, echoed back from the walls of the
tall, narrow old houses which cast dark shadows
over the alleys.

Phil came with me to the door of my room
and stood there chatting for a few moments before finally asking me if I would be free to join
him for coffee at the eleven o'clock break of the
morning conferences.

Although I guessed it was a second-hand invitation, because Sula would be busy with rehearsals all morning, nevertheless I was delighted to accept it.

The morning conference was interesting. I enjoyed my brief coffee with Phil, but what I enjoyed even more was attending Aldo's fashion show in the afternoon, because Phil slipped into the hall to sit beside me, no doubt to admire his beautiful girl friend as she showed off, along with the other pretty models, the variety of clothes for all occasions which Aldo had designed.

The highlight of the show was not the usual bridal scene, but a superb ballroom scene, in which the girls wore the most glamorous of evening dresses. The dress that Sula wore was the one which brought a standing ovation from the spectators, an ovation which had Aldo almost prancing with delight.

It was a ball gown in the old tradition, based on the gown worn by Emperor Franz Josef's beautiful Empress Elisabeth in the famous portrait by Winterhalter.

The foundation of glowing white satin was covered by a layer of white organza over the low, off the shoulder, tight-fitting bodice with its tiny puff sleeves, and layers and layers of organza flowed down from the nipped-in waist, cascading to the ground at the back like the froth of a waterfall. Tiny embroidered gold fleurs-de-lis glistened here and there all over the material, giving it a look of imperial luxury, and no one could have carried this magnificent creation better than Sula. She looked beautiful, with her glorious deep chestnut hair combed loosely out to fall over her bare shoulders, but kept back from her smooth forehead with a series of gold star clips. A superb necklet of rubies in an old-fashioned gold setting was the only piece of jewelry she wore.

"Isn't she lovely?" I turned impulsively to Phil, who, like everyone else in the room, had eyes only for the girl who held the stage.

He glanced at me and said with a shake of his head, "Sula always surprises me on an occasion like this. Usually, I see her, and think of her, as the wild young tomboy I grew up with and thought of as an annoying younger sister—the typical girl-next-door!"

"But you don't see her like that now?" I tried to repress a sigh.

"Sula will never change her nature," he smiled. "She is an extrovert, she loves showing off, and she is fun to be with, but," he shook his head, "I hope the man who marries her will realize what he is in for. Sula will lead him a merry dance. If he is the right man for her, he will enjoy it, otherwise," he shrugged, "I will feel sorry for him!"

I felt a sensation of delighted relief at his words. Phil was undeniably fond of the woman who laughed and smiled and blew kisses at the audience who were applauding her, but from what he had just said, it was plain he did not consider her as his future wife. The faint pangs of guilt I had been feeling about accepting his invitations to drink coffee together and to go sight-seeing together were stilled. I had no hesitation in saying yes when he asked me to join the Neilsons and himself at the opera that night, nor in accepting his suggestion that we should go to the Kunsthistorisches Museum the following afternoon.

Although I enjoyed the opera, Verdi's *La Traviata*, which is one of my favorites, I looked forward more eagerly to the visit to the Art Gallery. We would be on our own there, without Sula taking over the conversation.

When I was leaving the conference hall at lunchtime the following day, Karl Lippe, who had been loitering in the corridor outside, came hurrying across to speak to me.

"Fräulein Ogilvie, I understand that like us you have no meeting to attend this afternoon," he said, stopping in front of me.

"That's right," I smiled.

"Then I hope you will be free to join me for coffee at Demel's. It is a place I am told one must visit."

"I am sorry," I apologized, "but I have already arranged to go to the Kunsthistorisches Museum at three o'clock with a friend."

I was glad I had a genuine reason for my refusal, for I didn't fancy spending an entire afternoon in Karl's somewhat dreary company.

"Perhaps another time, *hein?*" he said hopefully.

I murmured politely that yes, that would be nice, and with a smiling goodbye, went off to join Mabel and Senga, who were waiting for me at the Hayden Café where we had arranged to meet for a snack lunch.

At three o'clock, dressed as usual in my warm coat and fur hat, I hurried down to the reception hall to meet Phil. He told me that since we didn't have a lot of time at our disposal, he had ordered a taxi to take us to the Art Gallery.

"I have to be back here at five o'clock," he explained.

There was a lot of scaffolding around the entrance to the museum, and great heavy pieces of tarpaulin, which had a leathery texture, hung down from overhead beams, completely covering the doorway. There was no one, not even a workman, to be seen, and we wondered if the place was closed.

However, Phil pushed a piece of the flapping tarpaulin aside and we found ourselves in a dark, shadowy, tented dome which covered the entrance steps leading to the great doorway, inside which we could see a man standing. Apart from the curators and their assistants there were few other people to be seen in the gallery on this cold November day.

Phil, like I myself, preferred to spend his time enjoying the works of a couple of artists, rather than trying to rush to all the rooms trying to glimpse everything at one visit.

We concentrated our attention on the paintings in the Breughel Gallery, and on the room alongside, which is given over to the works of Albrecht Dürer, although I wished there had been enough time even to glimpse the Velásquez collection.

When it was time for us to return we walked reluctantly back down the magnificent staircase, past the immense marble group of Theseus and the Centaur, to the lower floor, and out once again into the gloom of the tarpaulin-covered scaffolding.

I was a couple of feet in front of Phil, when he gave a shout and darted forward to grab at my arm and pull me back into the porch. At that very moment a beam from the shadowy darkness of the tenting overhead came crashing down on the spot where I would have been standing, knocking slivers from the stone steps with the force of its landing.

Phil was white-faced with anger and alarm as he stood holding me tight, and I was equally shaken, for this was the second time this week death had missed me by inches.

An anxious official came hurrying from the building to inquire if I was all right, and when he was assured that I had not been hurt, he went to examine the damage to the step.

Phil took my arm and hustled me past the official and the small crowd of people who had materialized at the sound of the crash.

"We'll take a taxi home," he said harshly, but there wasn't a cab in sight, so he hurried me across to a tram stop, where we stood shakily waiting for transport to arrive.

Phil held my arm tight as he muttered angrily, "I don't like what happened just now, Miranda. It could have been an accident, but again it could have been another deliberate attempt on your life, just as I feel sure that a deliberate attempt was made to run you down in Schönlaterngasse the other evening!"

His words took me so by surprise that I gaped at him.

"Phil! Don't be ridiculous!" I managed a shaky laugh. "Sula is right! She says that your profession makes you suspect everyone and every untoward incident!"

"My profession puts me on the alert for what seems wrong," he said gravely, "but what is more, I do have a genuine reason for believing that your life is in danger here in Vienna, Miranda!"

"Come off it, Phil!" I didn't know whether to be annoyed or amused by what he had said. "Who in Vienna has a grudge against me? Who, in his right mind, would want to kill me?"

He looked around, as if to make sure that there was no one within earshot, before he spoke again.

"Listen, my dear. What I am about to tell you, you must keep to yourself. I am only telling you what I know in order to put you on your guard against future 'accidents.'

"The truth is, Miranda, the police have now got evidence which proves that Ivy Sikorska didn't commit suicide, nor did she die of an accidental overdose of sleeping pills. She was murdered!"

I stared at him stupidly.

"Ivy? Murdered? But why? And how? And how do I come into it?"

"It was thanks to you that the murder was discovered," he said grimly. "Because you had cast some doubt on the sleeping pill theory, to be on the safe side, the police contacted their counterparts in Ivy's home town, to ask her druggist about the pils he had supplied. He confirmed his client never took tranquilizers of any kind. What he had prescribed for her was the medicine she always took when she went abroad, to prevent what she called 'Continental Tummy'!"

A tram came along and he ushered me aboard, saying, "I won't say any more here." He nudged me forward through the crowded carriage, and I had to contain my curiosity until we arrived back at the hotel and he came up to my room with me, so that he could explain his suspicions in privacy.

"The police theory is that Ivy actually did see her husband on the night of her death," he said, leaning against the edge of the desk while I removed my coat and hat and hurriedly tidied my hair.

"They believe he has assumed another identity, and could not take the risk of being recognized as Jan Sikorski! Ruthlessly he decided there and then his wife must be got rid of! He managed to obtain Ivy's room number, went along to see her, and naturally she let him in to talk things over. The police think he offered her a drink, doctored beforehand with an overdose of potent pills, which she swallowed while he looked on. To confirm the suicide or accidental death theory, he emptied away her own harmless medicine, placed a pill similar to the ones he had used to poison her inside, and left it beside her body for the authorities to find. He would have got away with it if it hadn't been for you, and your insistence that Ivy did not take sleeping pills!

"Dorinda Grey's accident is also suspect." Phil moved to a sitting position on the desk. "Remember, she had met Ivy's husband, and might also recognize him again! Although he didn't manage to kill her, at least he got her put out of harm's way in the hospital, where she would remain for the duration of his stay in Vienna, no doubt."

"Phil! You are making all this up!" I remonstrated.

"I wish I were, my dear," he shook his head, "but unfortunately, it is true that Ivy was murdered, and after what Ivy told you about her husband, describing how she had been able to recognize him immediately in spite of his changed appearance after over thirty years, you were put at risk too!"

"Phil, you are talking nonsense!" I persisted stubbornly.

"Miranda, you must take me seriously. What would help the police, and yourself, is if you could remember exactly what Ivy Sikorska told you that night. What peculiarity of his was it that made her so sure it was he?"

I sat down on the chair near him, and he looked down at me with an unblinking stare, as if he was trying to will my memory to return.

After a moment of silence, while I closed my eyes and tried to think back to the fateful night, I shook my head.

"It's no good, Phil. I can't remember. It could have been a scar," I bit my lip thoughtfully, "or

155

even a ring she had given him, or some mannerism . . ." My voice trailed off.

"The police here have got in touch with the RAF records department to see if they can get any information about Sikorski from them. They know he was posted missing after a raid over Berlin, and now they think he could have parachuted to safety somewhere behind the enemy lines and gone into hiding there, for he came down not far from his homeland."

"There are some Poles, both among our delegates and Sir Jack's crowd," I pointed out. "But what I don't understand is, why should I be in danger? Who apart from my immediate circle knew about my conversation with Ivy that night?"

"Ivy's death was news. People gossiped about it," he sighed. "Mabel, for instance, would have told Maurizio. He could have passed the news on to a friend of his, and so it goes, and rumor spreads like the ripples spreading out in the wake of a ship."

"It's too far-fetched, Phil," I protested.

"Nothing is too far-fetched in my business," he said grimly. "We have to consider every possibility, however remote, and your two recent, near-fatal accidents prove to me that your life is in danger. I do not believe in coincidences, especially when they occur conveniently!"

He slipped from the desk and stood up, looking down at me and saying, "So, my dear, please don't go wandering off anywhere on your own, and avoid lonely streets and dark corners. And don't—"

"I know!" I forced a smile. "Don't talk to strangers! My mother warned me against that a long time ago!"

"Her advice still holds good," he said soberly, walking towards the door. "I am sorry I have to go now, but I have my own job to attend to, and I must go and keep an eye on Sir Jack and his friends, and let my colleague have some freedom."

"I promised Mabel and Senga I would meet them in the coffee lounge at five." I glanced at my watch, amazed to find how late it was. "I'll just have time to comb my hair and pretty myself!"

"You look pretty enough to me," he twinkled down at me as I followed him to the door.

He paused on the threshold and smiled at me in a way that sent my pulse racing and made me forget the seriousness of what he had been telling me.

"Please keep a dance or two for me tonight, Miranda," he pleaded.

He continued to stare at me for a moment longer, almost as if he was reluctant to go about his business, then gently chucked me under the chin, saying, "Don't worry too much about what I have just told you. I shall try to keep an eye on you, as well as the lad my Austrian Police friend is going to appoint to watch over you!"

With that, he turned abruptly and stalked off down the corridor. I stared after him, my head cocked to one side as I tried to read a hopeful meaning about his feelings for me from his words and the odd, tender parting gesture.

Chapter Twelve

The women delegates at the conferences, much more so than the men, were full of excitement at the prospect of the Grand Ball which the government had arranged as a finale to the visit of their international guests of the week.

Over a late afternoon coffee in the Mahler Café, Senga and Mabel told me of a previous occasion which they had attended. The women went all-out to look their best, and the hotel's hair and beauty salons were fully booked from morning until they closed in the evening. Even the men, they told me, dressed up for the ball, so that it was like the lighthearted days of old Vienna, with dancing under the brilliant light of the many crystal chandeliers going on nonstop until the small hours of the morning. Several orchestras would take part, so that when one group stopped for a rest or refreshment, there was always another one ready to take over.

"The wine flows freely too," reminisced Mabel. "The Austrians are proud of the local selection they can offer—the Rheinrieslings, the Weissburgunders and Traminers—and if you really appreciate the local vintages, you will be offered a Grüne Veltliner, a Neuburger or a Zierfander.

"Ivy always enjoyed the final night of a conference to the full." Her tone saddened. "I still find it so hard to believe that she is dead. I didn't have much time for her, but she was a character, and she always provided us with something to talk about, even if it was just to exchange notes on how clever we had been to avoid her!"

"Let's not talk about Ivy now!" said Senga sharply. "I don't know why, but when you mentioned her name just now I had a fit of the jitters!" She shivered again. "It was as if mentioning her name was a kind of bad luck omen!"

"Don't be silly, Senga!" laughed Mabel. "You have so many superstitious omens, it's a wonder you aren't a bundle of nerves!"

She turned to me.

"Don't pay any attention to her, Miranda. You mustn't let anything spoil your enjoyment of tonight! It will be a memory you will keep all your days, for when you enter the ballroom, you will feel you have stepped back in time, to the Austria of the old empire, to the land of gaiety and waltztime and intrigue and romantic love; to the world of Klimt and Strauss and Lehar!" She sighed ecstatically. "I am always sorry when the dawn comes and we have to creep back to our rooms and pack our bags to return to home and the reality of everyday living!"

Senga nodded.

"After tonight, Miranda, when you see how lavishly we are entertained, as we have been entertained most of the week, for that matter, you will also appreciate why the old Prince de Ligne said of the Congress of Vienna which was trying to fix a peace treaty after the fall of Napoleon, 'The Congress doesn't advance—it dances!' But that is Vienna. A city of pleasure. A city with a special magic of its own."

If you were in love or having a light, happy flirtation as in the case of Mabel and Senga with their Italian and American colleagues, I could understand that the magic of Vienna would color everything with its dreamy romanticism, but if you had fallen hopelessly in love with someone; if you couldn't get that someone out of your thoughts, however hard you tried, and in spite of knowing that that someone was possibly in love with someone else, and would forget about you after tomorrow's final handshake and the final, insincere words which said how nice it was to have met, then Vienna's magic was a mockery.

"I bought a frivolous dress, especially for tonight!" Mabel chuckled. "The family thought I was quite mad when they saw it. They couldn't understand why a middle-aged mum would want to buy a ball gown for a single occasion!"

"I went to town on a new dress too!" sighed Senga. "I don't know when I shall ever have a chance to wear it again! Apart from these conferences, I never go anywhere special."

"I thought I heard Arnold say he was going to London for a holiday, and would look you up?" Mabel looked at her friend, her eyes bright with curiosity. "He's bound to take you out to dine and dance somewhere, so you will have a chance to wear it again!"

Senga flushed faintly, and without replying to Mabel, swiftly changed the conversation around to asking me if I had enjoyed my first conference with the Novelists Association.

"I wouldn't have enjoyed it so much if it hadn't been for you two," I told them. "You have fussed over me like a couple of older sisters, making sure I knew the ropes and didn't get left out of anything."

"It is rather a pity young Lippe is such a stiff stick of a man," sighed Senga. "He seems quite fascinated by you, but he is rather a bore, isn't he? At least," she added, "I find him heavy going."

"He tries to unbend, and he is most attentive when he is with me," I half-heartedly defended Karl.

"If Sula Neilson hadn't turned up, you might have made the grade with Phil Hunter," Mabel eyed me curiously. "He seemed quite interested in you that first evening."

Senga laughed and shook her head.

"Sula Neilson is not the kind of woman to let any man escape from her clutches without a fight. She knows how to flatter a man, and how to keep him thinking he is special to her, and," she shrugged, "there is no denying she is very lovely and has a lot of charm. It is a combination very few women can compete against."

"I rather like her," I put in. "I can understand why she is so popular, because apart from being attractive to look at, she is a most amusing companion!" I tried not to sigh with an onrush of self-pity as I finished speaking.

"I wonder what she will wear tonight?" mused

Mabel. "Something that will put the rest of us in the shade, no doubt!"

She signaled the waiter to bring the bill as she added, "Thank goodness you and I aren't in her age group, Senga. It must be most frustrating for the women who are trying to compete with her."

I thought dejectedly over Mabel's words as the elevator took me up to my room. Even if I had realized, before I left home, what a grand occasion tonight's ball was going to be, I couldn't have afforded—with the expense of the conference itself and the new winter coat and fur hat I had treated myself to—to splash out on an expensive new evening dress.

I pushed open the door of the wardrobe and considered the three evening dresses I had brought with me. Two of them I had already worn to the previous receptions, and the remaining one was the one I had thought most suitable for tonight's dance.

Now, remembering the eye-catching clothes Sula had worn at the fashion show yesterday, and having no doubts that she would be wearing something equally eye-catching tonight, I regarded my dress with a jaundiced eye. It was of nylon jersey with a softly draped V neckline. From the fitted waistband, the skirt dropped to ankle length, with narrow, unpressed pleats. I had bought it more for the hyacinth blue color of the material that was the exact shade of my eyes than for its style, although the easy, flowing lines of the skirt made it ideal for dancing.

Mabel had suggested that I go along to their

room when I was ready, so that we could go downstairs together to meet our partners in the cocktail bar.

I had tried not to look sorry for myself when they had been discussing their partners, for I foresaw that, as usual, I would be paired off with Sula's father or even Aldo Giovane, and although both men were pleasant enough and had been kind to me, they were much older than I was.

If only Phil Hunter had been unattached, I sighed to myself as I sprayed a mist of perfume behind my ears and on my wrists. I would have looked forward to the dance with delighted anticipation in that event. I remembered the foolish, lighthearted way he had taken me in his arms in the Stadtpark that first morning, only a few days ago in reality, although so much had happened since then that it seemed like months.

I closed my eyes and imagined his arms around me once again; imagined the warm feel of his hand in mine, our fingers intertwined as we waltzed crazily down the path; imagined the firmness of his arm around me as he held me close, spinning me into dizzy heights of happiness as we whirled around and around while he gaily hummed the music of a Strauss waltz.

The buzzing of the telephone on the bedside table interrupted my happy reverie.

"Miranda!" Senga spoke my name sharply. "We thought you must have fallen asleep! We have been waiting for you to arrive for the past ten minutes!"

"Oh!" I gasped, glancing at the clock beside

me. "I didn't realize how late it was! Senga, I am sorry to have kept you waiting. I shall be with you in a couple of seconds!"

I dropped the receiver back in its cradle, crossed the room to take a hasty glance at my reflection in the long mirror, grabbed up my evening bag and the mink jacket I had borrowed from my mother, and hurried from the room.

Senga and Mabel, both looking extremely elegant, were standing waiting for me outside the door of their room, and we walked along to the elevator together.

"Young Lippe won't be able to take his eyes off you tonight, Miranda!" Mabel smiled at me. "That dress is just perfect for you!"

I had been so caught up in my dreams of dancing with Phil that I had forgotten about Karl. Of course he would be at the ball as well, and it was more than likely that he would ask me to dance with him. My dress would remind him of the blue of his mother's eyes and of the blue of my own eyes, which had attracted him to me in the first place.

And Major Dietrich would be present tonight as well. I shivered with distaste at the thought. According to Karl, I also reminded the major of his lost love, so would he ask me to dance with him, because of this? Could I refuse him, if he did?

I felt chilled to the bone, in spite of the centrally heated atmosphere of the hotel, at the idea of being held in Dietrich's arms; at the thought of having to look into his cold grey eyes from a few inches' distance.

Now, thinking of the evening ahead, I experienced a curious sensation of uneasiness. I remembered how, earlier, Senga had felt the same way about tonight, because we had discussed Ivy in connection with the night's enjoyment, and I gave her a fleeting glance.

From the way she was chatting and smiling, it was plain that she had forgotten her disturbing premonition that something dire lay ahead this evening, but I myself could not throw off the strange mood which had taken hold of me, a mood which had been engendered by the inexplicable antipathy I felt for a man I hardly knew, a man who had actually done nothing to deserve my antipathy, which had been aroused, come to think of it, by Karl Lippe when he had given me a bitter account of his own attitude towards the man who had once loved his mother.

Although it had been originally arranged that we meet up with the others in the cocktail bar, there had been a change of plan, and we found them waiting for us at the entrance of the long, broad corridor which led past the ballroom.

Along one wall of this corridor a long line of tables had been arranged, set out with innumerable wine glasses and bottles of the numerous varieties of Austrian wines, and as the guests passed by to go into the ballroom, they were handed glasses of the wine of their choice by one of the many waiters in attendance.

Sula looked like an empress holding court as she stood in the hall, surrounded by the five men of our party, who seemed unable to drag their gaze from her.

She was wearing the glamorous Empress Elisabeth-style ball gown of white organza embroidered with tiny gold fleurs-de-lis which she had worn at the fashion parade, and her gleaming hair was spangled with gold sequins which danced and sparkled with each movement of her head. She was beautiful, and she knew it, just as she knew that she made every other woman in the company appear insipid in contrast.

"Thank goodness she has Phil to dance attendance on her," Mabel whispered to Senga. "At the same time, I have the feeling that even our old faithfuls will be queuing up for the chance to dance with her!"

When she saw us coming, Sula smiled in our direction before laying an imperious hand on Phil's arm, as a gesture that he could now lead her into the ballroom, where small tables and chairs were set around the edge of the well-waxed parquet floor which could accommodate several hundred dancers at a time without appearing overcrowded.

Already a number of couples were energetically moving around the vast space to the catchy strains of a modern cha-cha, and Sula and Phil joined them.

I danced with each of the men in our party in turn. Arnold Weissman was a mediocre dancer, but his witty conversation as we moved around the room made up for the number of times he trod on my toes.

Maurizio Lenno held me very close to him, dancing cheek to cheek, as he did with all his partners. Sir Jack was an accomplished dancer, and I enjoyed the modern waltz we partnered each other for.

When the orchestra struck the opening notes of "Tales from the Vienna Woods," Phil Hunter rose to his feet with alacrity and took hold of my hand, pulling me up alongside of him and saying with a pleasant lilt in his voice, "This is definitely our dance, Miranda!"

The expression in his eyes as he spoke made my heart skip a beat, for he was looking at me as if he genuinely wanted to take me in his arms and dance with me, and was not merely asking me for *noblesse oblige.*

I thrilled to the touch of the firm hand which grasped my waist, and, afraid that he might guess the intensity of the pleasure I was experiencing, I half-closed my eyes as we circled the floor, so that I could enjoy, without betraying my feelings by the expression in their depths, the happiness I felt as he held me tight, whirling me around and around to the music, looking down at me with a smile on his lips, but making no effort to talk to me.

I was so entranced with the delight of the moment that I sighed when the music came to an end and Phil led me back to our table.

His arm, still circling my waist as he guided me across the floor, seemed to tighten its clasp as he looked down at me and said, smiling, "We dance well together, Miranda, don't we? So please," he begged, "keep the next waltz for me!"

Before I could answer him, Sula, who, with Aldo, was walking from the floor alongside us, took hold of Phil's free arm and said petulantly, "That's not fair! You haven't waltzed with me yet, Phil!"

"And you haven't danced a polka with me yet!" laughed Aldo, catching me by the hand and pulling me back to the middle of the hall, as the orchestra played the opening chords of the merry "Tritsch Tratsch Polka."

Aldo was as light as thistledown on his feet, a truly superb dancer. We cavorted spiritedly around the room, and I do not think I have ever enjoyed a polka as I did that evening! I was laughing and breathless when we finally returned to our table, and I still hadn't fully recovered from the energetic dance when Karl Lippe came striding across the hall towards me, and with stiff formality asked me if I would honor him by dancing with him.

I hadn't the heart to refuse.

Phil was fastening the catch at the back of Sula's dress and did not look up as I followed Karl to the floor, but Sula winked at me and seemed amused at the attraction I had for the shy young physicist. I pretended not to notice her look as he took me in his arms to the strains of the romantic "Blue Tango."

Unfortunately Karl's dancing prowess was not equal to the subtleties of the tango. His movements were as jerky as those of a marionette whose strings are pulled by an inexperienced puppeteer, he had no ear for music, and he could not quite keep in step with the beat.

I felt awkward and self-conscious as we moved stiltedly around the hall, occasionally bumping into other couples, and I was glad that the hall was crowded so that we were hidden from Sula's mocking gaze, although I had the unhappy feeling that she might be mischievous enough to encourage Phil to dance alongside us, if she did happen to spot us.

We moved past the table where the East German party was seated. Dietrich's chair was half turned away from the floor, and he did not appear to notice us, as Karl stumbled awkwardly yet again in his endeavor to hurry away from his colleagues.

After we had almost completed one circuit of the ballroom, Karl decided he had had enough and steered me to the edge of the floor, near the open window which led into a small courtyard where, in the light streaming through the window, the little white round iron tables and chairs which would be used for sitting outside in the warmer weather gleamed like forlorn ghosts.

"Miranda, I do not dance very well. Forgive me!" Karl looked down at me and I could see the perspiration, like small crystals, sparkle on his forehead.

"Karl, the tango is not the easiest of dances!" I found an excuse for him.

"No dance is easy for me!" he said, glancing around as he took me by the arm to stand beside a tall, spreading palm. "I do not enjoy dancing, but I wanted a chance to be with you!" His face turned a deep scarlet as he was speaking, and I felt sorry for his gaucherie.

"Tomorrow, Miranda," he continued, "I go home. I shall not see you again. So," he hesitated, "tonight let us talk together, *hein*? Let us walk in the cold night air, away from all this," he grimaced at the bright lights, the revolving dancers, the sound of music. "Let us do what I used to do as a child, with my mother," his voice grew strained. "We used to go to a stall at the corner of our street, on a frosty night, and buy hot chestnuts, or our favorite sausages—"

"What do you mean, Karl?" I asked, puzzled.

"There is such a stall here, at the other side of the park across the road from the Mahler. When I saw it, it reminded me of home," he sighed. "It is not far!"

"Karl! Really!" I laughed, pooh-poohing the idea.

"M-M-Miranda, p-p-please!" he stuttered. "It would m-make me so h-happy, to do this with you!"

I hesitated. Across the ballroom, I caught a glimpse of Sula and Phil, reflected in one of the high, gilt-framed mirrors which lined the far wall, dancing cheek to cheek.

No one would notice if I slipped away with Karl, and in any case, it was no one's business but my own what I did. In a way I felt sorry for Karl and his homesickness, and what was more, if I left the ballroom now I would not have the disappointment I was sure was in store for me. When the next old-fashioned waltz was announced, and Sula claimed it with Phil, in spite of his half-promise that we should dance it together, my pride would be saved by my absence, and Phil would be saved any embarrassment.

"P-please, Miranda!" Karl coaxed again,

wiping his forehead where the beads of perspiration were gathering in still greater profusion. "It would be so pleasant to spend a short time with you, away from Major Dietrich's constant supervision!" he added as he glanced surreptitiously to the table where his colleagues were sitting.

Looking at him, I sensed what an effort it had been for him to make his proposal, and it was this which finally decided me.

"Very well, Karl," I replied briskly. "But I shall have to go back to my table to get my fur jacket."

I was on the point of moving away, when he caught me by the arm.

"Wait!" he whispered. "The major is watching us. If he saw us leave together, he would follow and stop me!"

His eyes glittered strangely as he continued in a more determined tone, "I tell you what we shall do! I shall return to my friends. When I do, you can leave the hall, and I shall follow you in a few minutes and meet you across the road from the hotel, in the entrance to the park!"

He gave a harsh laugh as he added, "It is like a conspiracy from one of the books you write, *ja*?"

Poor Karl. I shook my head as I watched him return to his friends. What sort of life was it, when you were not free to talk to whomever you wanted, and had to go to such silly lengths to date a girl?

I returned to my table, picked up my fur jacket and left the ballroom, and as I walked down the passage towards the reception hall, the strains of the haunting tango throbbed faintly in my ears.

I stopped beside the desk to put on my jacket, and when I approached the main exit, the night porter held the door open for me and asked, if I wanted him to hail a taxi for me.

"No, thanks!" I smiled at him. "I am merely going across the road to join a friend!"

Seeing the knowing look in his eyes, I added hastily, "We are going to your famous stall by the park to sample some more of your Viennese delicacies, before we leave Vienna tomorrow!"

I don't think he believed me, for he gave me another odd look. On the other hand, he may have been surprised that my friend had not had the courtesy to come to the hotel to meet me.

However, I ignored his suspicious glances and walked past him, to stand hesitant on the pavement outside, waiting for a car which was speeding down the road, to drive past.

When its tail lights disappeared around the corner, I glanced up and down the road once more, to make sure there was no more traffic in sight. After what had happened the other evening, I had become very chary of crossing the Vienna streets!

As I looked around, I caught a glimpse of a man, wearing one of the tall fur cossack hats which Karl affected, slipping out from the side entrance of the hotel, further down the road, and go hurrying across the broad street to where I had agreed to meet Karl in the deep shadows cast by the trees.

Chapter Thirteen

Although there was only a light breeze this evening, the night air was decidedly chilly. Patches
of near-freezing fog festooned the branches of
the trees by the park gate, softening their win-
ter-bare silhouettes and drifting so thickly
around the lower part of their trunks and along
the path which led into the park that they
seemed to be hanging in air rather than rooted
to the ground.

The softly swirling mists, changing pattern
with each puff of wind, gave the scene a sepul-
chral look, as if they were shrouds drifting down
to cover the corpse of the winter-dead earth.

I shivered at my imaginative thoughts. I was
on my way to meet a young man at the Viennese equivalent of a hot dog stall, so why think
in gloomy terms of death, when an amusing in-
terlude lay ahead for me. For an instant there
flashed into my mind Phil's warning about going
off on my own, but I instantly rejected it. I
wasn't actually on my own now, for Karl was
waiting for me just across the street, and if there
was any danger to me from anyone, which I still
doubted, it would be from Ivy's husband, and he
wasn't young and blonde, but grey-haired and
past middle age.

All the same, I cast a glance back into the
well-lit entrance porch of the Mahler, where the
porter was still regarding me with a worried

frown over the shoulder of a smaller man who had come over to speak to him.

If I hesitated on the edge of the pavement any longer, he would no doubt read into my actions something more disreputable than a foolish desire to sample hot food from a stall on a cold street corner, especially when I could have gratified my hunger in the warm comfort of the Mahler Grill.

Snuggling my coat more closely around me, I turned away from his gaze and went hurrying across the road towards the park gate.

Karl had moved right into the park, where the tunnel formed by the branches of the trees blotted out the street lighting. All I could see of him was a shapeless figure, his coat collar turned up against the cold, his tall fur hat pulled well down over his forehead, so that the only part of his face which was visible to me was the lightness of the whites of his eyes.

"Come!" he muttered gruffly, and took me by the arm in a grip so fierce that I winced at the pressure of his fingers. I wriggled my arm to indicate that he should ease his hold of me, but he only held me the tighter as he propelled me down the path so quickly that I almost had to run to keep up the pace he set.

"Karl, for goodness' sake!" I gasped. "What's the hurry? Even if Dietrich notices that you have slipped from the ballroom, he will have no idea where to look for you!"

The man laughed harshly. "Nor for you, my dear!" His voice grated roughly, and it was as if a stranger were speaking.

"Karl!" I protested with growing anger as he made no effort to slow down. "This is carrying your childish conspiracy to the point of absurdity! I can't keep up this pace with my high heels, and the ground is slippery too!" I let out a wail as my foot skidded on a pile of slimy leaves.

Only my companion's iron grip saved me from sprawling backwards to an undignified seat on the ground, and for that at least I had to be grateful to him.

We plunged still further into the park. From the trees overhead, pearls of ice-cold water dripped onto my face, making me shiver; and unseen in the mists which writhed around the shrubberies I could hear night creatures moving. I started in fear as a huge bird, disturbed by our approach, swooped down, making me duck instinctively before it winged its way back to its perch.

I could now hear the sound of running water, and I frowned. This could only mean that we had moved back to the Wienfluss, instead of away from it.

"Karl! You have taken the wrong turning! You should have gone to the right, not the left! We will soon be back where we started from!"

Again I tried to pull myself free, and again my companion laughed his disconcerting laugh and urged me on, his hold on me so firm and iron-hard that I might have been a prisoner in custody.

My high heel caught on an exposed tree root and I tripped, but again I was prevented from falling as I was dragged on, with never a pause in our onward rush.

Anger was now giving way to a growing fear. Karl was behaving most oddly. He had uttered a mere half-dozen words since we met, and now he was behaving like a robot, a creature who had been wound up to perform a certain act and would go ahead with its program no matter what happened. A man who behaved as he was behaving now could not be quite normal! What on earth had I let myself in for, I wondered, trying to control a tremor of fear.

We passed under a drooping willow tree near the bridge where Phil and I had seen the police congregate on our return walk through the park, after our first outing together. The mist-wet sprays of the osier trailed slimily across my face and tangled with my hair.

"Karl! Stop!" I cried furiously. "This is as far as I am going! You can go and eat your stupid chestnuts or sausages by yourself! I am returning to the hotel!"

"Yes, my dear!" Once again he uttered his strange, malevolent laugh. "This is as far as you are going!"

He stopped abruptly as we emerged from the drooping willow branches, but retained his hurtful hold of my arm.

"Then let go of me!" I cried, and tried to wrench my arm away, but still he held me tight.

"Really, Karl! This is too much!" I ejaculated, turning to look at his face, which was now faintly visible in the light cast by the street lamps on the other side of the bridge.

As I gaped at the man who was holding me, a scream rose to my throat, to be clamped back as he rammed a rolled-up handkerchief into my mouth with his free hand. I found myself staring petrified not at Karl Lippe, but at a much older man whose face twitched with excitement, and whose nervous tic made his left eyelid droop lower and lower, until it completely hid the murderous expression in the eye it covered.

Now, too late, the memory of Ivy's description of her husband's peculiar nervous trait came back to me, and with it the knowledge that the police were right. Ivy Sikorska's death had been murder. Dorinda Grey's accident had been no accident, but a further attempt to get rid of someone who might identify him for who he really was, and now I, myself, because somehow he had learned that I knew of his treacherous mannerism, and might talk of it, was doomed to die! I knew there was no appeal to clemency. This was a man who acted ruthlessly to get what he wanted or to save his skin.

As an animal instinctively lashes out to try to save itself, I tried to kick out at Ivy's murderer, but he dodged aside and then, twisting my arm with such brutal force that I writhed with pain, he frogmarched me towards the water's edge with one hand, while with the other he slowly and deliberately pulled the white silk evening scarf from around his neck.

"I see you recognize me now!" he said softly, menacingly. "And you will understand why I have to kill you. Why, like the chambermaid who saw me leave my dear wife's room the night

177

I killed her, you have to be got rid of! Think of the disgrace for me, if you lived to tell your story!" His voice grew hoarse with rage. "I killed once, a long time ago, to start my new life, and I shall kill again, to keep it. No silly women, like Ivy, like the little maid, like you yourself, are going to spoil things for me. It would be ridiculous to let you try, *hein?*"

Still holding me with one hand, he tried to make a running noose with his scarf with the other, and all the time he kept speaking.

"No one will ever suspect me of anything! Ivy's death has already been dismissed as an overdose taken in error by a woman who was too intoxicated to know what she was doing. Dorinda Grey's accident, which will keep her out of the way until I leave Vienna, has been accepted as just that. As for you, young woman," he muttered an oath as the silk knot slipped away and he had to try once more to make a noose, "as for you," he repeated, his setback making him vent further spleen on me by giving my arm another vicious twist, "like the silly little chambermaid who arranged to meet me in the park, because she thought I was going to spend money on her, and take her to a night club, you will be seen to be another victim of the same murderer. And I," he pushed me to my knees and dangled the noose over my drooping head, "I shall go on as heretofore, respected, kowtowed to because I am who I am, or rather, should I say, who I have become since the war ended!"

As the silk of the scarf touched my hair, I jerked my head quickly to one side, knocking

178

the slippery weapon from his hand and taking him by surprise with my action, so that he momentarily eased his grip.

I tried to struggle to my feet, my right hand tugging at the gag which had been stuffed into my mouth, and I had just managed to pull it out when he knocked me roughly to my knees again and flung himself on top of me so that his full weight was on the back of my legs, which stuck out behind me.

His grasping hands felt for my neck and closed around my throat, while I pulled desperately at the clutching fingers, scraping viciously at the backs of his hands, then at his cheeks with my long, sharp fingernails.

He screamed in pain as a nail caught in the corner of his eye, and for a moment his grip slackened, but when I tried once more to pull his hands from my throat, his rage overcame his pain and he renewed his pressure on my neck until my head felt as if it was going to burst with the agony of it.

It was all over now, I knew. I closed my eyes against the final moment, and then, strangely, the compression on my throat eased, and I could gulp for breath.

Through the giddy mists of faintness which threatened to engulf me still, I heard Sikorski utter a vile profanity in his own language, as he pushed me aside and struggled to his feet. At the same moment I heard what he had heard seconds earlier—the sound of running footsteps drawing near to us, the click of shoes on stone, and men's voices shouting a warning.

In a final attempt to get rid of me, my assailant lashed out at my head with his booted foot, but I rolled to one side and the very force of his movement made him lose his balance on the icy path. He struggled to keep on his feet and I rolled further out of harm's way, croaking as I did so to the dark, shadowy figures who came racing down the path along which, only seconds ago, I had been so painfully propelled.

"Help me! Help! *Hilfe! Hilfe!*"

The figures materialized into definite shapes—a half dozen men—two policemen in uniform, the officer who was a friend of Phil, the man I had seen talking to the night porter, Major Dietrich and Phil Hunter.

The policemen went racing after Sikorski, but Phil and Dietrich came running to me and helped me to my feet.

"Miranda! You little idiot!" Phil blazed at me in anger. "I told you to go nowhere on your own! Surely you realized the danger you were in from what I told you this afternoon!"

Even in the dim light I could see that his face was paler than usual, his expression tense and strained as he demanded harshly, "What made you come to the park on your own, Miranda? What on earth possessed you to do such a tomfool thing?"

"Phil!" I could only whisper my answer because of my aching throat. "I wasn't going to be on my own! I had arranged to meet Karl on the other side of the road!"

Phil seemed unaware that I had spoken. He put his hands on my shoulders, and holding me at arm's length he stared at me intently in the misty luminosity of the street lamp on the other side of the bridge. His anger gave way to concern as he asked anxiously, "Did he hurt you, my dear?" His voice was shaky. "Are you all right?"

"My throat!" I touched my neck gently. "He tried to strangle me! He— oh Phil!" I choked. "It was terrifying. He wanted to kill me! I thought—" I gulped, and could say no more.

"My poor darling!" Phil moved closer to me and his arms dropped to my waist, holding me close, and I clung to him, my head against his shoulder, sniffing tearfully with relief.

"It's all right, Miranda," he whispered reassuringly. "It's all over now. He won't get away. He'll never harm anyone again."

"He will harm his wife!" said Dietrich harshly. "Or rather the poor woman who thinks of herself as his wife. My dear Berta!" he shook his head in anger. "How will she be able to bear this scandal he has brought on her, and on her son!"

As I clung to Phil, unwilling to leave the safety of his arms, Dietrich turned to me.

"There is one thing none of us can understand, Fräulein Ogilvie. Why did you come to meet Lippe—Sikorski—here, in the park? You had never spoken to him. He, for his part, ignored you completely, so how did you arrange the meeting, and why?"

I pushed myself away from Phil and faced the major.

"It was Karl, not his father, I arranged to meet at the park gate. He wanted me to go with

181

him to the stall where they sell chestnuts and sausages. He was nostalgic about the memory of doing this with his mother, when he was a small boy. I felt sorry for him, and I saw no harm in falling in with his whim."

"But when did he arrange this?" demanded Dietrich, raising his voice so that it could be heard above the noisy shrilling of police whistles and nearby angry shouts.

"It was when we were dancing the tango," I told him. "Karl said he felt hot, and we stopped near the window. Then he suggested a walk in the cool night air along to the stall—"

Dietrich frowned. "I don't understand. I saw him take his leave of you in the middle of the dance, and then he returned to our table and immediately asked Fräulein Mund to dance with him!"

"That's funny!" I shook my head. "He said I was to leave first, and he would follow, since you might suspect we were up to something if we left together."

"His father excused himself the moment Karl reached the table," Dietrich frowned. "They must have arranged the thing together, but why?"

"I think you can guess at the answer, major," said Phil grimly.

"But I don't understand!" I looked from one man to the other. "It doesn't make sense!"

"I'm afraid it does, Miranda," said Phil slowly. "But the explanation is too long and involved to tell you here and now."

He put his arm around me once again in a

gentle, protective gesture, and instinctively I moved closer to him, enjoying the feeling of safety and security he engendered, as we walked back to the hotel. Dietrich and the police officer came hurrying back to us to tell us that Sikorski had been caught and was on his way to the police station.

I was discreetly hustled through the reception hall of the Mahler and up to my room in such a way that the other guests had no time to notice the disarray of my hair, my colorless face, and the stains and tears on my evening gown.

The police took a statement from me, and then said that in order to make the minimum of fuss and to keep international relations on their usual friendly basis, they would be obliged if I said nothing about my ordeal to any of my friends.

They then sent for a doctor to examine my throat, neck and mouth, but apart from faint bruise marks, which he told me might look even worse in the morning, and a cut on my lip made when Lippe had rammed the handkerchief into my mouth, I had physically escaped remarkably lightly from the attempt on my life.

However, I was advised to take a hot bath and get to bed and given a sedative pill to calm my overwrought nerves.

Phil, who had been waiting outside the bedroom for the doctor to leave, came in to find out if there was anything he could do for me. When I assured him there was nothing I needed, he promised to return in the morning with full details of the case, saying he would be able to answer all the questions which must be buzzing around in my mind by then.

As we said good night at the doorway, he took me lightly in his arms and brushed his lips against my forehead in a feathery kiss.

It was the thought of Phil's gentleness and kindness, and the delightful memory of that unexpected kiss that soothed me more than any pill a doctor could have prescribed. I fell asleep, to dream that the tenderness he had shown towards me was for someone he cared for, and not merely because he felt sorry that I had been the victim of such a trying ordeal.

Chapter Fourteen

True to his word, Phil Hunter telephoned me at nine o'clock the following morning to ask if I had slept well.

"I hope your throat isn't too painful and that you can swallow your breakfast coffee without difficulty," he added.

"The waiter has just this moment arrived with my tray, so I haven't had time to test what it is like to eat anything."

"How about asking the waiter to bring an extra pot of coffee and an extra cup, and I shall join you for breakfast, and at the same time fill you in on most of the facts about Jan Sikorski's masquerade and the events of the past few days?"

"Since I woke up, I've been trying to work things out for myself, but there is a lot I don't understand and I would be very interested to know how he worked his scheme. In any case," I added happily, "it would be nice to have company for breakfast. I don't like eating alone."

As we drank cup after cup of coffee, Phil told me that Sikorski had confessed to his past and present crimes almost as if, now that he had been caught and there was no way of escape for him, no place he could even escape to, he wanted everyone to know how he had fooled the world for over thirty years.

Sikorski's mother had been German, his father Polish, and they lived in a small town near the German-Polish border. Just across the border, in Germany, lived his German aunt and uncle, who had a son, Jan Lippe, a year younger than he was. There was a certain family rivalry, for both boys were very clever. Both were sent to University, Sikorski to Warsaw, Lippe to Berlin, and they studied similar sciences.

At the outbreak of World War Two, Sikorski was called up by the Polish Army, his cousin Lippe by the Germans. Sikorski escaped to England with many other Polish officers when his country was overrun, and there he trained with the RAF to become a navigator. It was during his training period that he met Ivy, then a pretty and vivacious young woman. Sikorski was impressed with the fact that she too was a University graduate, for in his country it was usually only the daughters of the rich who could afford to go to college. He was also impressed by the large, rambling house she lived in, not realizing that it was the vicarage and did not belong to her father, and even more impressed when he learned that her uncle-by-marriage was a lord and a member of the government.

Ivy's own vivid imagination about herself and her family and how wonderful they were added in his illusion that he had married a wealthy and influential wife, but after almost five years of marriage he had found out that things were not as he had hoped them to be.

On one of the final air raids over Berlin, the plane in which he was navigator was shot down, but he managed to parachute to safety. He landed not far from the village where his uncle and aunt lived, and he decided to make for there and plead asylum for old time's sake. However, he knew that as a Pole who had fought for Britain he would be far from popular if he was arrested on his way, so he removed his uniform and dressed himself in clothes stolen from a lonely farmhouse. Speaking German as fluently as he spoke his native Polish, and knowing the countryside well from holidays spent there in his youth, he was able to reach his uncle's village, only to find it completely devastated in the fighting.

An old man, grubbing in the ruins of a house near what was left of his uncle's home, told him that all the Lippes, including Jan, who had been home on leave at the time, had been killed. He was the only one left alive in the village, for he had been out in the woods looking for firewood when the battle had swept through the little town only a week earlier.

Quick-thinking as always, Sikorski saw his

chance. He had no desire to return to England. If he was caught in Germany as Sikorski, he would be shot, but if he managed to survive, using his dead cousin's name, there might be a new future for him. His mind made up, he had no qualms in killing the old man who would be the only person who knew that the real Lippe was dead, and he was sufficiently like his cousin in appearance and knew enough about his background to pose as him in a different part of Germany.

After the war he settled in East Germany, where he met Karl's mother. She was the daughter of a leading government official, and he realized that as a member of such a family no one would ever dare breathe any suspicions of him, should any such suspicions arise. He charmed her away from Dietrich, her then fiancé, married her, and returned to the studies which war had interrupted to prove himself one of the most brilliant physicists in the country.

Life went well for him until the unfortunate day Ivy recognized him in the elevator. His son was with him when Ivy made her very positive identification, and when they left the elevator, Karl asked for an explanation. It had gratified some instinct in Sikorski to tell his son the truth. He knew Karl could not give him away, at the risk of a heartbreaking scandal for the mother he adored. After all, as Ivy's husband, Sikorski could not be legally married to Berta, which made Karl himself illegitimate. Karl's pride would not stand having the world know this, so Sikorski had a willing accomplice to help him in his plan to remove the woman who was a threat to the happiness of them both. Apparently he had not been quite so willing when it came to planning my demise, but he realized the inevitability of it if he wished to keep his father's secret from his mother.

Major Dietrich had apparently always been suspicious of Sikorski's background, from some chance remark he had made confusing his period at Warsaw University with that of his cousin's at Berlin. His suspicions had been maintained, since he was sure that Sikorski did not love the woman the major loved, and had merely charmed her into marrying him for his own ends. Dietrich was afraid for Berta's future happiness.

It was the coincidence of the International Physicists Conference and the International Novelists Conference taking place in the same hotel in Vienna on the same week, which had been reponsible for Sikorski's downfall. Even then he might have got away with Ivy's murder and the murder of the chambermaid if Ivy hadn't mentioned to me her antipathy for sleeping pills, which had set the machinery of police investigation into motion.

In a way I felt sorry for poor Karl Lippe, who had been caught up in a web of deceit and murder from which he could not escape. I felt sorry, too, for the murder victims and for poor Dorinda, who would have to remain in the hospital for another couple of weeks at least. But the person I felt most sorry for was Karl's mother. She had done no one any harm, but now she had lost both husband and son and her life was in ruins.

When he had finished telling me the full story and we had drunk the final cups of coffee from the pots the waiter had brought us, Phil put his hand on mine and said gently, "Miranda, I know you have had a most frightening experience, and that you must still be feeling very upset, but do you think you could bear to walk through the Stadtpark with me again this morning?"

"Do you want to try a kind of therapy?" I asked shakily.

"You could say that!" He smiled and walked over to the wardrobe to fetch my coat and hat. "Actually it is something I would like you to do."

There was a lightness in his tone which I could not understand, and I shot him a puzzled look as he helped me on with my coat and stood watching while I carefully pulled my hat over my head.

There were not many people in the reception hall as we walked across to the swing glass doors, where the day porter wished us a pleasant "*Grüss Gott.*"

However, I could not repress a shudder as we entered the park at the same place where I had entered it the previous night, for what had almost been a rendezvous with death. Seeing my tremor, Phil took hold of my arm and held me close. He smiled down at me, and the moment of fear passed.

Now we were treading the path we had walked along on our first morning together, but today a crisp frost hardened the ground so that the leaves were brittle and not damp underfoot, and our breath patterned the air in front of us like smoke puffs.

We reached the open-air orchestra stand, and Phil stopped and looked at me. His eyes were smiling. His mouth was smiling. The day itself seemed to smile as he held my gaze.

"Miranda, darling Miranda!" his voice lilted as he spoke. "This is where I first took you in my arms. This is where I first felt attracted to you, as no other woman has attracted me, and that attraction keeps on growing!"

I looked at him, my eyes shining, a flush of happiness warming my cheeks as he continued:

"So much has happened in so short a time, Miranda. So much tragedy, so much excitement, so much fear. Now I want you to put all the unpleasantness behind you. I want you, when you think of me and of Vienna, to remember only the happy times. I would even like to think that ahead of us there will be many happy tomorrows.

"In fact, my darling, what I want to do is to begin all over again, from the afternoon of our lovely day in the Vienna Woods, and what better way to begin again than for me to claim the waltz you promised me last night. The waltz we never had."

He held out his arms to me, humming the opening notes of the tune that was to be our special song over the years, and as I danced around and around the little square in front of the bandstand, my cheek against Phil's, it was as if we were making a fresh start, or more truly, entering into a newer, more intimate relationship.

I laughed aloud, and the breath of my laughter rose like smoke in the air and was caught by the sunlight, which turned it into a coil of gold, and even though two great crows swooped and whirled overhead, they were no longer birds of ill omen. They were the birds of the old country saw I had learned as a child: One for sorrow, two for joy—and today was going to be a very joyous day!

"I shall be flying home with you," Phil smiled down at me, "and believe it or not, I have found out that I live only a couple of hours by car from your home town, so you aren't going to get rid of me easily, Miranda!" he teased, knowing from the look in my eyes, which reflected the look in his own, that I didn't want, ever, to get rid of him.

I sighed blissfully as we danced over the fallen leaves, watched by curious-eyed blackbirds and sparrows and a couple of amused path sweepers.

I was the happiest, luckiest woman in the world this crisp bright winter morning.

The magic of the old Habsburg capital had worked for me, and what more could I ask at this moment than to be here, dancing in Phil's arms, and to be falling in love, in Vienna?